# GABRIEL'S LYRE

By Simon Ludgate

# Gareth

Gareth needs to take a leak. This would be unremarkable if it weren't for the fact he can only move his eyes and the index finger of his right hand. He has suffered from locked-in syndrome, total body paralysis, since the age of ten. He is twenty two years old now. He requires assistance. Again.

Voices, raised in argument, make it very loud in the Mercedes Traveliner. What started out as a discussion is escalating into a full-blown argument. It drowns out the engine and road noise.

One of those voices belongs to Rula, a human rights lawyer from Israel, who suddenly raps the flat of her immaculately-manicured hand on her clipboard.

"We have been over this so many times Robin. Why can't you get it into your head? The State of Israel's claim to that area dates right back as far as the days of the Hittites and the Pharisees. The children of Israel laid claim to Jerusalem two thousand years ago."

From the front, little Robin, a Palestinian, swivels round and bores her brown eyes, which are so dark they are almost black, into Rula's face which is almost completely hidden behind oversized dark glasses.

"See—that is just so much bullshit. Lord Rothschild did a deal behind our back, the first of many, with the west in 1914. It was called the Balfour Treaty and it

1

sold the land which Israel claims, illegally, as theirs to-day."

The stunning dawn breaking over the Scottish Highlands whips past unnoticed.

Gareth tries to get their attention.

"Guys, I need to pee."

His tinny voice synthesiser has a flat, expressionless monotone.

Trent, Gareth's father, drives with a determined set to his strong jaw. His clenched teeth and furrowed brow are born out of familiarity with the argument. He's heard it all before. Who was there first? Who wasn't? No one can really remember. Which is precisely the problem and the basis of the circular argument he's heard his friends have a thousand times?

Robin is warming to her theme.

"So have you ever heard of the Khazars?"

"You mean the Mongol horde from Russia who converted to Judaism and settled in what is now Israel?" sniffs Rula.

"They are your true ancestors, right there. Scholars have been battling it out over this for decades. And it's never even been proven that the children of Judea ever existed."

Robin coils round, a look of triumph on her eye-catching, chiselled face. Game, set and match. At least that's what she thinks.

"Well that's where you're wrong."

Rula sits forward to pursue her argument with the small, muscular woman in the front seat.

"I've read about that scholarly argument about our origins. It's history versus genetics right? The Koran tells similar stories from the same eras. Stories of angels and demons."

Gareth has switched on the headlights built into the ends of the wheelchair's arms. Trent notices the beams in the rear-view mirror.

"Guys, can you take a break from arguing for a minute? I think Gareth needs something."

Ted, a huge, bearded man of Apache descent, leans over the back seat to where Gareth is parked in his wheelchair.

"What up Cochise?"

"I just need a leak. Can we stop for a minute?" drones Gareth's voice synthesiser on one note.

Ted turns toward Trent and taps him on the shoulder.

"Trent? Pull over dude. Gareth needs a pit stop."

Trent hoves to in a layby. The process to get Gareth out of his wheelchair begins. The rear door clicks open and starts to rise automatically. A metal ramp extends from the rear of the specially-modified people carrier until it reaches a metre behind the vehicle.

Ted, mahogany-dark, who wears his hair long like the Apache Brave he is, and Eli, a tall, handsome, muscular man whose deep tan is as much at odds with the chilly, grey Highlands of Scotland as Ted's appearance, step forward from either side of the people carrier. They reach in and clear the pile of rucksacks and climbing gear which has almost buried Gareth in order he can get out.

Gareth whirrs forward onto the extended plate on the all-wheel drive buggy. He has clearly done this many times before as his movements are quick and precise. From the front Trent lowers Gareth to the road using a control on the driver's console. It beeps confirmation as the metal plate touches the ground.

Gareth wheels off it and rolls round the back of the people carrier. He halts by the kerb and waits for Ted and Eli to catch up. Gareth is motionless and implacable. He is in a permanent state of full body paralysis brought on by the stroke he suffered when he was just twelve years old.

Weakened artery walls tore in his neck and blood seeped into the bridge, the Pons, between his brain stem and the main lobes. Before anyone realised what the cause was, Gareth fitted then collapsed. It was the last time he experienced movement of his own volition. Once he was stabilised, he was put in an induced coma in the hope it would give his body time to recover while he was in a controlled state.

Doctors could tell he wasn't a cabbage from his brain activity on the ECG but the MRI scans revealed a poor prognosis. At best they thought he might regain partial or full control of his motor functions at some stage in the future but so far, ten years on, he has only learned to control his eye movement and his right index finger.

Ted gently raises the fighter-pilot style gadget over Gareth's right eye which he uses for controlling the wheelchair. He releases the bright red five-point racing harness Gareth insisted they used so it would match the smart black Recaro Racing bucket seat.

Eli's muscles bunch and the tattoos across his arms and shoulders squirrel around as he and Ted lift Gareth out of the chair. They point him into the freezing wind whipping across the purple heather of the beautiful, barren vista.

Rula is pretending not to watch the well-practised ritual. Her eyes narrow with curiosity.

"God help us if he wants to take a shit."

The wind catches Gareth's stream of urine and blows it back across them.

"Goddamit," grunts Eli. "Ted—other way dude!"

Ted and Eli swivel Gareth through ninety degrees, and then back again, in a futile attempt to second guess the gusting wind. Curious heads turn away in the people carrier as one so as not to embarrass Gareth even more.

There really isn't anything left to dehumanise my life any further, Gareth thinks to himself.

Gareth does a lot of thinking. He remembers when he read The Outsider by a German writer called Franz Kafka at school for his GCSE exam. It was about a man who wakes up one day and finds he has turned into a beetle. The theme was about exploring alienation. He likes that word—alien-ation. Or should it be Alien Nation? Gareth feels like both—like an alien and alienated.

I have no friends, he realises. You can't exactly hang out with your locked-in syndrome buddies. For a start there aren't many of them and who wants a mirror held up to what is, in reality, a life sentence? Anyway, Gareth would rather just mix with able-bodied well, girls, really. As would any other twenty two year-old guy who prefers the company of girls.

Being suspended while he wets himself in an arctic wind doesn't rank amongst the most fun things to be doing. And the audience pretending not to watch doesn't help. To distract himself, he thinks about who he would kill first. It's nothing malicious but when you can't move a muscle, some pretty strange thoughts enter your mind.

But if he were to kill them, not that he would *really* you understand, he'd start with the males. Eli first. He's the most dangerous as he's the strongest. And he's a trained killer. Which he respects. A professional. A US Marine who saw action in Afghanistan.

Anyone who can deal with a rope suspended from a helicopter as they slide toward the ground in pitch dark, in enemy territory, has to be a great ally but equally a hard to kill enemy.

Then it would have to be Trent, his own father. An ex-combat veteran like Eli, Trent was a British troop transport helicopter pilot who flew Chinooks in Afghanistan. Gareth's step-mother, Rachel, met Trent while he was in therapy for post-traumatic stress disorder. She was his therapist. Gareth's real mother, Delissa, killed herself 12 years ago. Although he can't remember how. But then he can't remember much. Trent, Rachel and Delissa—what a fucking fuckfest.

Ted, although an imposing man physically, is not capable of harming anyone, Gareth decides. He is into tracking and using his sixth sense so he would more likely jump off a ledge than harm me. Marine engineer turned prison services officer. A screw to you and me. A correctional officer according to Ted.

But respect to the guy. Apparently he looked after some of the meanest. One inmate required six officers every time they went in his cell. He had this trick where he could smash the steel door of his cell from its hinges by swinging at it repeatedly while hanging from the heating pipes. Burnt his hands red raw each time he did it but he didn't feel it.

The strangest thing about Ted is his obsession with his hair. He honestly believes it has magical qualities like Samson in the Bible. Samson lost all his strength and superpowers when they cut off his long hair and Ted actually believes all that shit. Ted says his hair is an extension of his nervous system and it's his radar. Total wacko.

Robin. Underestimate her and you'd be dead, that's for sure. Although she can't exactly reach the top shelf, she knows how to kill someone with her bare hands and where she grew up in the Gaza Strip, you needed to know how to. Her best friend was shot by Israeli border guards who mistook her for a suicide bomber. At the age of eight.

They shot her eight times as it happened. Once for each year of her short life. In the hearing conducted by the Israeli internal investigation body she was referred to repeatedly as "The Package". They found themselves not guilty. Just doing their job and, hey, after all it has been known to happen. Kids used as suicide bombers. She just kept coming towards them and wouldn't stop.

But the truth was she couldn't understand what they were shouting and was terrified of all the guns pointing at her. She thought they were ordering her to approach. In fact they were telling her to stop. But she just kept coming, her hands raised in the air. So they shot her.

But Robin would have to be next. A tiny trained killer with a grudge.

Rula you could take out any time, thinks Gareth as they load him back into the Mercedes. He hadn't realised the role killing played in the mix. Such fucked up lives, all of them.

But Rula would eventually talk you to death so he would have to kill her anyway, just to shut her up.

And she is his step mum Rachel's bestie, so that qualifies her for despatch right there anyway.

Game over. None of them would ever know how close they came.

Trent pulls out of the parking spot and settles back

into an easy pace as they head toward the big blue mountains in the distance. The ancestral seat of the Laird of Bothy in the Cairngorm mountains. One of the highest and, at times, the most desolate places in Scotland.

During the dark winter months when the snow is piled into soft, clinging drifts by the biting wind blowing down from the Siberian Arctic in Russia, the area seems as remote—and cold—as the moon.

Even now, in the height of summer, the wind has an Arctic sting and there is what feels like snow hanging in the clouds. Climbing in mid-summer when the days are long and it is supposed to be balmy was a dead cert for some great R n' R when Trent booked the trip in January.

"Do you think we have enough warm clothes?" Trent asks out loud to no one in particular.

Rachel, Trent's wife and Gareth's stepmom, an elegant beauty with shoulder-length rich brown shiny hair, appraises the pile of gear in the back next to Gareth. Climbing pitons and caribiners clank against metal water bottles, spoons and tin pots.

"We've packed for warm-weather climbs. Perhaps we should have brought cold weather gear. It feels like it might snow."

"What did I say before we left?" Trent can't help himself.

"Let me see. You said something like whatever we take will be wrong, so we should pack the opposite of what we think we'll need was about the gist of it," smiles Rachel, although the smile doesn't reach her eyes.

"So why didn't you make me follow my own advice?" asks Trent, goading his wife.

"Because it's always a double bluff with you my darling. I always forget I have to tell you to do the opposite of what you say," sighs Rachel with a mixture of resignation and irritation.

Rula, in the third front seat, breaks in.

"So let me make sure I've got this right. Trent announces his theory, and then you have to have him to do the opposite, because if you don't it's your fault and he blames you?"

Trent says nothing and stares through the windshield.

After a long, uncomfortable silence, they come to a fork in the road.

"I think the turning to the castle is coming up," Trent grunts, more for something to diffuse the antagonism in the air than for any other reason.

Gareth stares out of the rear window. His eyes focus on something behind the people carrier. As they rush past in the van, two crows, which are perched on either side of the road like black Centurions, flap into the air. The sinister-looking birds follow the vehicle at a distance of about twenty metres.

As the Mercedes slows and swings right up the side road which leads to the castle, the crows turn and follow them. Gareth watches for a while as they continue to flap behind. They neither increase nor decrease their distance.

"We've got company." He drones through the voice synthesiser attached to his wasted vocal chords. Ted is the only one within earshot.

"What up dude?" asks Ted as he turns his bulk toward Gareth.

The crows are gone.

"Nothing. It doesn't matter."

# Laird Of Bothy

They are approaching the castle. Built by the first Laird in 1800, it is an imposing edifice made from Scottish slate. Its tall, thin cone-shaped turrets are a grand gesture towards castles built by the Normans when they took control of England in the 12th century.

The gravel drive is long and sweeping. It is a grand place with an air of solidity and permanence. Birds have made the nooks and crannies of the roof their home. They rise reluctantly into the air in twos and threes screeching a complaint because their peace has been disturbed.

As they approach the castle, Trent slows to a halt.

A line of civilian vehicles are parked in front of the castle. Some have bits of smoking junk from an explosion scattered across them. Although it is deserted and there is no welcoming party, no one can have left as the castle is miles from anywhere. The nearest village is five miles down the approach road—the only road leading to Bothy Castle.

"What the hell is that?" Trent asks, pointing.

A large military vehicle discarded some way from the group of parked vehicles has been blown to pieces. Debris is spread across the gravel drive. Nondescript bits of automobile are scattered every. What remains of the Humvee, a massive-wheeled five-metre long, very tough, off-road staple of the US army, is still smoking slightly.

A black scorch mark runs along the
Whatever caused it has split the canvas in
tattered sections.

For once, there is silence in the people ca.11er.

"Looks like the Gaza Strip," Robin says drily.

"We should take a look around. The Laird was supposed to be meeting us but God knows what's happened," grunts Trent.

"I was thinking more waiters in suits with trays of
drinks. Kilts. Scottish pipers. That sort of thing. Not
this." Robin wrinkles up her nose.

Eli, Trent and Robin walk cautiously to the main
entrance. Ted and Rachel pick a careful path through
the smouldering wreckage surrounding the blown-up
Humvee.

Distracted 100 percent by the sight of the destroyed
vehicle, they forget Gareth. He is still in the back of the
people carrier. Gareth's eyes swivel as he watches Ted
and Rachel walking through the debris.

"What about me? You forgot me." Gareth's tinny
plea goes unheard.

Then, from somewhere deep in the castle, music
starts to play. A stringed instrument picks out a rippling
cascade of notes which rise and fall in pitch.

"Suddenly getting a whole lot weirder," whispers
Robin to herself in a sing-song voice.

"There is something very not right here."

Trent's ability to state the obvious is in overdrive.

"Not right at all," agrees Eli. He unsheathes the ra-
zor-sharp hunting knife strapped to his thigh where an
army-issue Smith and Wesson sidearm would have once
hung.

"At least we know someone is around and they are

ve enough to play a harp," offers Trent.

The gently rising and falling cadence of the harp hangs on the wind coiling around the cold grey slate walls and towers.

From where she and Ted are standing amongst the wreckage, Rachel sees Trent and the others disappear into the castle through its Gothic front door. A gargoyle sits astride the entrance, its head in its hands and its tongue poking out.

Rachel looks up and is struck by the demonic-looking stone statue.

"That thing would be more at home on a parapet of the Notre Dame Cathedral in Paris," she says nervously.

The longer she stares at it, the more it seems to be directing its insolence at her. Her head starts to buzz slightly and the ground is starting to swim around. She staggers and almost falls. Intuitively, Ted spins around and catches her just in time, hauling her up by an elbow. He looks at her then refocuses his gaze more deeply as if he has sensed something he hasn't felt before.

"You OK? You ain't pregnant or nothing are you?"

She looks at him blankly then shakes her head. "Huh? No. Impossible. Hey we left Gareth behind."

The electric rear door and the ramp whirr into action simultaneously. Gareth wheels forward as soon as he is able. Intrigued, he heads straight to the Humvee to investigate immediately he is clear. He's never seen a dead body and this could be his chance.

"The music's stopped," observes Rachel, her head cocked to one side.

"Maybe Trent has found the source," replies Ted.

Rachel and Ted make their way to the entrance and

disappear inside. Gareth is too absorbed in the wreckage of the Humvee to notice. He moves around the still-smoking carnage and stops frequently to study the damage. What has been going on here, he thinks to himself.

Gareth takes stock of the situation. We are on a rubbish climbing holiday—rubbish because no one seems to have noticed or care that I won't exactly be abseiling down anything—and we've gone from boring tedium to complete weirdness in five seconds. How is that even possible?

We rock up to what is supposed to be headquarters for my whacked-out dad and my clingy stepmom's climbing love fest and what do we see? Post-traumatic stress disorder triggers a go-go scattered everywhere like psycho-therapy chunks of bullshit. Well Rachel will have a field day that's for sure.

Her swanky cognitive behavioural therapy degree will no doubt get a right airing after this. That's how she met my dear old dad in the first place after all—trying to cure his PTSD after two tours of Afghanistan.

Going down in a big old rig like a Chinook and almost getting captured can't have been particularly nice. Taliban rocket propelled grenade through the rear rotor then spinning into the ground with a crew of three and five injured squaddies on board. Everyone dies except you.

How guilty is that going to make you feel? Big time self-loathing and angst.

And then your wife kills herself when you get home. But it wasn't our fault was it? Despite what the doctors and everyone else qualified to wear a white coat and look serious said. I can't even remember what she looked like now. Delissa. My mother. Did I love her?

Did she love me and Greg? Who knows?

But I wonder who died here? Gareth's fixation with death balloons to occupy his whole mind. Someone did for sure. Cars don't just blow up on their own do they? It takes effort. Explosives. Somebody wanted to hurt someone. Despite being convinced there has to be at least one dead body, there are no smoking, charred corpses in the wreckage of the Humvee to be seen. No trace of casualties. Not one whiff. Disappointed, Gareth bumps and lurches after the others.

As he passes under the sinister gargoyle, Gareth stops and stares at the demonic-looking figure above the arched doorway. It could be rebellion or it could be fear. Only Gareth knows what emotion is registered as his implacable face can't relay any clues.

"Anyone read a book called 'Gormenghast'?" he asks out loud to himself as he enters the gloom of the castle interior.

That's the thing about locked in syndrome. You can still feel sensation. You can feel if someone pinches you or the toilet is required. Quadriplegics have a bag to piss into. It just happens without you knowing. But extreme cases like me, thinks Gareth, have the strangest life. I'm firing on all cylinders in my head and lower down. I could be dead. Except I'm not. I'm alive in here. They seem to forget that sometimes. All I can do is stare at the idiots. Most of them seem to have less going on in their minds and bodies than I do.

Gareth stops in the enormous echoing hall. His eye flickers around, illuminated more clearly now in the relative darkness by the baleful green glow of the transparent plastic finger in front of his eye. The Recaro Racing seat is identical to the body-hugging cocoons fitted in endurance racing machines which compete in the legendary 24 Hours of Le Man and World Rally Competition. Gareth is fanatical about racing. In fact he is addicted to anything dangerous. The black seat almost encloses his atrophied body completely. It curves round his head like a Nylon flying buttress. Ideal for stopping his head from flopping around.

In racing the elephant ears of the seat are designed to prevent whiplash in a sudden impact with a wall, but it serves equally well to protect Gareth. The black racing seat and his bright red five point harness are a dramatic contrast. Very new and very smart. Gareth loves it. A gift from the Mobility Charity. Ten years of being frozen like a statue changes your priorities in life in ways other people can't begin to understand.

The Great Hall is spectacular. Broadswords, armour and tapestries almost cover the impassive grey slate walls completely. Where the slate has been rendered with plaster there are paintings of the Laird's ancestors. Proud, fierce and warlike, you wouldn't want to pick a fight with any of them. History, especially military history, is Gareth's other passion apart from racing cars. Something he inherited from his father, Trent, who won't even talk about the army these days.

This refusal by his father infuriates Gareth more than anything. Light a fire under someone then walk away. What's the point of that? The greatest gift Gareth can conceive is being able to heft one of those huge swords on the walls of the Great Hall in his hands and clash with the enemy. Imagine the damage a five foot razor sharp blade could inflict.

Gareth is not quite so enamoured by the stuffed stags' heads. Their glass eyes follow him as he trundles forward to avoid their deathly, glassy stares.

He imagines sighting down a hunting rifle in the

stillness of a winter's dawn with an alpha male stag in his crosshairs. Slowly squeezing the trigger and then watching the huge lead slug of the bullet arcing away towards the head of the magnificent animal. Yes, you can actually see the bullet flying through the air away from you, he's been told by proponents of the art.

Thunk! It enters the skull, drills through the brain and compresses. Turning from a projectile the size and shape of a magic marker to a flat brain mashing disc, it decelerates through the animal's head and bursts out through the back in a spray of red mist.

A magnificent, beautiful animal the same weight as a small car buckles at the knees and goes down, dead before it hits the ground. That's power.

That's also disgusting. How can taking a life be so exciting and repugnant in equal measure?

He wouldn't the want the stag to stay dead. He would want it to get up and trot off unharmed and safe. But then that's the dilemma with killing. It's exciting thinking about it, doing it even. But what do you do with a huge, lifeless form? Gareth is relieved he will never have to experience the confusion caused by the joy of killing and the guilt of the consequences.

To Gareth's astonishment, the memory of his mother Delissa floats into his mind. The expression on her face as she lay broken and lifeless at the bottom of the stairs.

He realises that is the only recollection he has. His memory of her is blank otherwise. Gareth can recall his twin Greg in three-dimensional detail. They were identical and inseparable.

"Phone's dead," says Trent.

"Use your mobile you idiot," chides Rachel.

"Do you think I haven't thought of that?" snaps Trent. "I tried that outside but there's no signal and no landline working. Great."

Trent slams down the receiver in disgust.

"It's OK Trent. We just drove here. I can drive out just as easily," says Ted nonchalantly.

"Yeah, no biggie. We can all get right back in the Merc and hightail out of here," adds Eli.

"I'm not sure that's such a good idea," replies Trent. "It's getting dark."

He walks to the window and looks outside. The wind has picked up and rain has started to pop against the glass and the skylights in single large gobs.

"It's going to come down big time. We've been driving for eight hours and we've got Gareth to consider," Trent states.

"I agree. Gareth gets sick when he can't get enough rest," says Rachel as she bends to touch Gareth's head.

He scoots away. In his haste to escape from Rachel, he bumps into the central breakfast island in the kitchen by accident.

Rula has been observing the domestic debate silently until now.

"I don't mean to be rude, or selfish for that matter, but are you all out of your tiny fricking minds? Are you *seriously* contemplating staying the night in this creepy place?"

"Rula's right, Trent. There is no explanation for that mess outside. Whatever has taken place is not healthy we can be sure of that. I'd bet my shirt someone died in the process," agrees Ted as he unconsciously moves closer to Rula.

Gareth's wheelchair rotates on its axis. The headlights built into the arms switch on and are bright pencils of light in the increasing gloom.

"Who died?" rasps his voice synthesiser.

"Ah Gareth. Come and join in the discussion darling," responds Rachel as she folds her arms and sinks back on the kitchen island. "What would you like to do? Stay or go?"

Gareth whirrs forward and rotates his wheelchair to direct the pencil beams at his step-mother.

"I vote we stay. I'm tired. People have died. More might later. Where do I sleep? And who was playing the harp thing?"

"Switch your headlights off darling, there's a good boy," sighs Rachel.

The lights flick off, then back on for a rebellious second, then off again.

"We don't know that Gareth," says Robin quietly. "But you're right. We're safe here. There's no sign of anyone dead. Maybe the lorry outside had a fault and the petrol tank exploded and they've gone to get help. Maybe it's something simple like that."

At that moment the lights go out, leaving them standing in the kitchen in near darkness.

"Oh, that's just great," shouts Ted with irritation. "That clinches it. I'll take the Merc and find someone to help. There must be a police station near here. Did anyone notice?"

Robin produces a map and spreads it out on the breakfast island. Ted and Trent snap on their climbing headlamps so they can study it. Gareth switches on his headlights too but the sudden glare at chest level blinds everyone.

"Gareth I know you're just trying to be helpful but could you stop doing that?" snaps Rachel.

"Get off the kid's case, Rach. That wheelchair cost a small fortune and he's still learning what it can do," counters Trent.

"Maybe we could plug him into the castle and run the lights off his batteries?" suggests Robin.

"This is serious," Rula is unravelling. "You might find this funny but we are looking at no hot water I assume, a freezing cold night and having to walk around this creepy old house in darkness. Let's just go. Come on it's obvious."

Ted stabs a huge finger into the map.

"Found that sucker. Aviemore Police Station and it's got a mountain rescue centre too. That figures. OK—I'm gone. Who's coming?"

Rula and Robin exchange glances. Robin tilts her head at Ted and winks at Rula.

"I think Ted needs a bit of legal protection on his journey. You go with him Rula. By the time you get back we'll have cooked some dinner and figured out how to make the best of this mess. Bring us a nice big Scottish bobby."

"Wouldn't it make more sense to take Trent or Eli with me? I could do with another guy to back me up."

Ted looks to Trent and Eli for support but he doesn't get it. Judging by how much Rula is blushing, no one presently has any inclination to stand in the way of true love.

Muttering under his breath in disgust, Ted walks towards the door but stops and waits.

"So are you coming or not lawyer woman?"

Rula swings her handbag over her shoulder and picks up a torch which she switches on and waves in Ted's face.

"Oh alright then, someone needs to stop you from

falling in a ditch."

🎵🎵🎵

The night has submerged the castle in inky black. Ted is thinking about darkness as he leaves the relative safety of the murky womb-like gloom of the great hall. Its animal head trophies take on a more sinister aspect with the absence of daylight. Darkness has come to embrace the human race every day since time began. A rhythm imprinted on the human psyche literally as sure as night follows day. One of the great certainties in life.

But what if that certainty were to end?

Tonight.

For some reason which he doesn't understand, all of Ted's natural self-belief deserts him in that moment as he and Rula walk out of the grand main entrance under the gargoyle. It holds silent vigil over the darkness as it has for two hundred years. But what if this was his last night on earth? He would have no idea. He could have woken up this morning, anticipating a relaxing holiday with friends only for it to be his last.

Does anyone have a presentiment of their own death? Even someone as intuitive as him. Who wakes up and thinks "I'll die today?" What on earth is making me think like this he wonders. But it's gone. The certainty of more, of being. It feels as if his ego has been sucked from his body like an egg thief emptying a prized shell of its contents through a pinprick-sized hole. The shell is left perfectly intact but the contents have gone. That's how he feels. Something he has never once in his life experienced.

Ted's sense that he is going to die, and soon, is overpoweringly strong.

"Ted are you alright?"

Startled, Ted is snapped back from his reverie. Rula is standing close to him in the darkness. She is studying his face which is broadcasting his momentary crisis.

"I'm fine. It's just..."

Ted for once is lost for words.

"Are you uncomfortable about being with me?" probes Rula on completely the wrong track.

"No way, no," Ted stutters. "I mean, why? No I just had a thought, that's all."

"I'll inform the media immediately," Rula cracks back.

Ted half shudders, half shakes his massive bearded head and shoulders in an attempt to slough off the strange mood which has suddenly engulfed him as he makes for the people carrier in which they arrived. It's still unlocked from their earlier stunned exit after coming across the burnt-out Humvee. Ted hefts himself into the driver's seat. Rula gets in the passenger side and then folds her arms expectantly.

Ted reaches for the keys in the ignition in an automatic gesture but they are not there.

"What the fuck has Trent done with the keys?" he snorts.

Without saying a word, Rula reaches over and dips the sun visor. The keys drop into his lap.

"Smartarse."

Ted smiles sheepishly at Rula.

"Anytime," Rula leans back and recrosses her arms.

"Come on then."

She cocks her head expectantly.

Ted turns the key. Nothing. The Merc sits impassively with no apparent interest in going anywhere.

"That's odd," says Ted dumbfounded. "What the hell's wrong with it?"

"You won't get any sense out of me I'm afraid. I don't do cars," shrugs Rula. "Maybe if you look at the engine you will spot something."

"Oh that will work. Definitely."

Despite the sarcasm, Ted gets out again and lifts the hood. He does exactly what Rula suggested and looks at the engine as if he's expecting a part of it to have vanished.

"Well?" asks Rula impatiently.

Ted shrugs and raises his hands.

"Someone must have left the lights on or something."

"OK well if our vehicle is dead, what about one of the others? They look more suitable anyway. Let's try one of them instead."

Rula is already heading for the old Land Rover parked next to the Merc. A farmer's chariot like a land Rover wouldn't even need a road to get away from the castle. They would be able to drive it right across the fields if they had to.

By the time Ted reaches the old four-wheel drive, Rula is behind the wheel. She hits the ignition. Dead.

"Oh come on!" Rula smacks the big Bakelite wheel with her palms in frustration. "Not this one as well?"

"Maybe it's been standing for a while. I'll try one of the others." Ted ambles off.

He makes his way down the line of five more vehicles. They are all rugged off roaders designed to be driven through snow or deep standing water. Not one has a spark of energy. Every engine is comatose and utterly disinterested in showing any sign of life.

The sense of dread and faceless fear returns to Ted's belly and he is suddenly aware of how intensely cold it is. He notices Rula is shivering as she stands in the darkness.

"We better go back inside and give them the good news."

"I'd—h-h-h-hardly—c-c-c-c-call it good." Rula can barely spit the words out between shivers.

"It is good. Means we get to all stay here together tonight in such a fine example of Scottish heritage," says Ted a lot more brightly than he feels.

Trent has his head in the fridge when they return to the kitchen. He straightens up and snorts in disgust. He has a flashlight in one hand and a dark chunk of something in the other.

"This ham looks, and smells, like it's been in there for months. So does everything else in the fridge. Disgusting."

He computes the fact Ted and Rula are back in the kitchen a mite too soon after they left to get help.

"You were quick. Where are the cavalry?"

Ted bristles at the implied criticism.

"They're not coming Trent. Every vehicle out there is like they've all had the battery stolen. We couldn't get a single one going and I'm fucked if I'm walking five miles in the dark in this temperature. Rula was freezing her tits off five feet from the front door."

Rula clips Ted round the back of the head.

"Nice image. Thanks."

It's clear no one is going anywhere for a while. Robin, Eli and Rachel make themselves busy tidying up the mess in the kitchen. Decomposed food fills the fridge. Using the light from the assortment of wind-up camping lights they have brought with them they clean up the debris and bag it.

Trent, Ted and Rula make their way around the first and second floors of the castle and allocate rooms to everyone. The deepening darkness and lack of electric light has transformed the interior of the castle into an assault course of twisting staircases, sharp edges and unforgiving stone floors. The paintings of the Laird's ancestors seem to watch them impassively as they stumble around in the dark.

Gareth watches the clean-up operation impassively. Eventually he fires up his headlights and practices rotating his wheelchair through 360 degrees right, then left. He perfects being able to rotate right round without drifting off centre. He spins faster and faster while he holds position by using the brake on one wheel. The wheelchair suddenly lurches off to the side and he crashes into a cupboard which bursts open. An ironing board and an aluminium kitchen stepladder clatter across his lap.

Gareth sits motionless while the ironing board and the ladder slide across him and strike the floor, blocking any potential exit. Like a joke without a punchline Gareth continues to stare unemotionally at the cupboard. Eli gently untangles Gareth from the wreckage then leans down really close to Gareth's ear. They are both lit by the green light from the slim piece of Perspex which curves round Gareth's face, covering his eye.

"It's OK Cochise. I don't think anyone noticed. You're in the clear."

Using cans of food from the cupboard, Rachel creates a sort of tuna and tomato stew with a few tins of assorted beans and pulses thrown in. The gas cooker range is unaffected by the power cut, apart from an inability to ignite, so matches are struck to light all five gas hobs. One for the stew, one for the beans and the rest to counteract the deepening chill. Instinctively everyone gathers around the source of heat and light while the food is warming.

"Smells good," sniffs Ted.

"I hope it's OK. It's all we could find. There's enough to last another night, maybe two," Rachel says uncertainly.

"Two nights staying in Castle Dracula? You are kidding me. If we have to walk out of here, that is what we are going to do." Rachel's eyes are shining in the glow from the cooker.

"And what about Gareth?" asks Trent evenly. "We have already been through this. We can't leave unless we have transport for Gareth too. He can't just up and leave."

Gareth whirrs forward into the glow of light from the cooker.

"I am actually in the room too you know?" he says in his flat synthesised voice.

"We haven't forgotten you Gareth," sympathises Rachel.

"No, you're the reason we're going to spend the night here Gareth. And everyone should be glad we are as it's the most sensible thing we could have done," states Trent flatly.

The looks on the faces of the others don't support Trent's statement.

Then the sound of the harp is there again. A rising and lowering cascade, played deliberately and slowly, over and over.

Everyone freezes.

Gareth is the first to speak. "There is someone else here. I knew it!"

"If they're here we will find them," barks Trent as he grabs a wind-up lamp. He strides across the pool of light thrown by the cooker and disappears into the gloom.

Over his shoulder he shouts, "Ted—Eli, see what you can find upstairs. I'll search the ground floor and outside. Robin and Rula—see if there's anything around the back door. Rachel—you stay here." Then he is gone into the darkness.

Gareth swings round to follow his father. Rachel steps across his path.

"Stay here with me Gareth. I need protecting."

Gareth stops. Step-mother and step-son contemplate one another.

"If you think I'm falling for that, think again," intones Gareth's voicebox.

They look at each other. Neither speaks.

"What happened to Greg, Rachel?" asks Gareth.

There is another long silence while Rachel weighs up a response.

"This is not the right time, Gareth."

Gareth is silent but his eyes glisten slightly. Rachel can't interpret the emotion. Anger? Sadness? Recrimination? It's not a conversation she is going to have now, not here. Too difficult. Her counsellor mind engages. Not something to talk about while life is taking such a weird turn. The sound of the harp stops.

"Thank fuck. That's better. I am getting really freaked out," Gareth still has eyes fixed on his step-mother.

"Gareth are you OK? Why are you staring at me like that?" she asks.

"Like what?" Gareth replies blankly then whirrs away from Rachel right out of the kitchen, leaving Rachel alone. She is motionless for a few seconds as she goes over the awkward conversation she just had with

Gareth, and then she snaps out of it and stirs the tuna and tomato stew.

The others reappear a few moments later. No one is any the wiser. The castle has been searched from end to end and revealed nothing.

What had started out as a group of friends on the first day of a relaxed climbing holiday has turned into six scared, isolated individuals with no idea whatsoever how or why that's happened.

🎵🎵🎵

Trent and Rachel are in bed.

Lying in Trent's arms, Rachel has her head on his chest as much for warmth as physical comfort.

"Christ it's cold in here. I knew I should have packed a blow heater," Rachel whispers as she hugs Trent tighter.

"Wouldn't have done you much good would it with no power? I'm enjoying the experience though," he replies.

"You would wouldn't you?" She studies her husband's strong face. "Are you OK?"

"OK as in happy OK or post-traumatic stress disorder OK?" Trent is teasing her again.

"You should at least take my diagnosis as your CBT counsellor seriously."

"The only thing I take seriously is the fact that coming to you for counselling after we got shot down in Helmand province resulted in us being together. It's the us together part which means so much to me. You know how I feel about lying on a couch talking about myself."

"Trent, that's exactly what I mean. We made so much progress with coming to terms with what happened, losing colleagues, and the guilt after the crash."

"Guilt? It was no one's fault, certainly not mine. We've been over this."

Suddenly angry, Trent pulls away from Rachel and turns on his side. Rachel stares at his back for a few moments then she slips into the curve of his back and hips.

She rests her hand on his arm and whispers, "Just promise me one thing. When it comes to my turn to die, I want you holding my hand. Promise me."

Trent rolls over to face his wife and he kisses her gently on the mouth.

"I promise," he whispers back.

# Deep of the night

The night has transformed the castle from a haven into a dark place full of threat and menace. The only sound, apart from the eerie whistling of the wind which blows down the chimneys above each of the four massive fireplaces on the ground floor, is the metronomic tick of a clock.

The three foot long clock pendulum swings to and fro in its casket. The clock emits a loud mechanical tick as each second passes. Its huge brass fascia contains a sun and moon which rotate slowly.

The ticking echoes throughout the drafty main hall. It feels like everyone's dead for real now, thinks Gareth to himself. He whirrs into the hall by the main entrance. Gareth doesn't sleep at normal times. In fact he doesn't sleep much at all and when he does his eyes often forget to shut.

I must look really dead then he thinks to himself. Rachel puts drop in his eyes every day because of that and forgetting to blink which irrigates the eyeballs naturally. She's OK really. Just not his mother, even though she does a pretty good impression of one. The pretender to the throne.

Trent has bought in that's for sure. He's swapped one addiction for another. The high and adrenaline of flying on the front line for the high of being in love. Can't get much better than that. Or maybe that should be can't get much worse than that?

Gareth is an incongruous sight as he moves almost silently around amongst the hunting trophies and the oddly unsettling paintings of previous Lairds of Bothy, kings, rebels and leaders of the Scottish people who fought against the invading English.

Finding a depiction of the battle of Culloden, he reads how in 1746 some dude called the Duke of Cumberland mustered an English force and confronted the Scottish rebels. I suppose they were what would be referred to as terrorists or freedom fighters these days depending on your perspective he thinks.

Gareth imagines the sounds of battle as the English and Scottish faced each other across the boggy marsh in the illustration. Two thin lines of different clans of the same race charging towards one another to greet certain death. The English cavalry apparently sneaked round and charged between small groups of Scottish fighters—farmers and labourers mainly—and hacked them to death.

After most of the heavily-outnumbered and out-fought Scottish were chased off the field of battle, those who hadn't been slaughtered where they stood fled and tried to hide. But the murderous Duke had other ideas. He ordered his men to seek them all out and most were killed in cold blood where they were hiding.

Too weak and exhausted to offer much resistance, the Scots were hacked to bits. Now here's the really outrageous bit thinks Gareth as he is reading. The Duke carried on the killing to include anyone else he could find in the area. Women and children weren't spared it seems, according to the narrative text accompanying the pictures.

The Duke had been ordered by the King to put an end to what was considered an "uprising" in London by the ruling classes and he took him at his word. He'd seen the Scots fighters succeed in part against the English forces, who were a long way from home, and unsure about what they were doing there in the first place.

The display finishes by pointing out the battle at Culloden was the last one the Scots fought against the English and thereafter were in their power which led to the present day one nation under one flag.

"Well that won't last," Gareth says aloud.

As his words die away there is a deep, unearthly, ironic laugh from somewhere. Although Gareth is not capable of any movement he has a full set of senses and he feels the hairs on his arms and neck stand up as a cold fear snakes through his whole body. He flicks on his headlights and spins round. There's no one there.

Suddenly Gareth really wants to be with his parents so he directs his wheelchair to the bottom of the stairs which leads up to where they are sleeping.

"Help. Dad, Rachel. Can you hear me?"

His voice synthesiser sounds puny in the black silence.

"Hello. Shit."

He waits for a reaction but none comes. Rivulets of sweat trickle down his forehead and into his eyes. Sweat is the worst. It itches and tickles and there is nothing he can do about it.

Giving up, he whirrs on further in a series of circles as he checks for whatever enormous beast is coming for him at any moment. He heads away from the stairs and motors round the back of them. The headlights pick out a set of what look like a warehouse freight elevator. Gareth, forgetting there is a power cut, crams up against the wire of the elevator car. He is looking for the button which will open it and provide sanctuary from the horrible noise he just heard.

There it is!

He extends the probe in the right wheelchair arm. The slim titanium rod has a rubber button on the end and Gareth makes several stabs at the call button. Still terrified by the sudden deeply horrible noise he just heard, Gareth's frantic movements with the probe, combined with fidgeting the wheels of his chariot, fail to land a successful depression of the button.

He backs up slightly and stops. A few seconds pass, and then a few more. Gareth rolls forward again towards the elevator. As he does so the safety cage opens as if someone has done the job for him.

He still hasn't successfully pressed the button.

Gareth pauses for a moment on the threshold between the dark void and the familiar solid ground of the hallway. He rolls inside. The safety cage drops as if by magic—normally it would take a strong manual heave to pull it upwards or back down—and Gareth sees there is just one operating button and that's marked 'Down'.

But the elevator must have used the last of whatever stored mechanical energy it had left to open, as it now starts to head downwards in an accelerating and uncontrolled drop. Cables whine and rattle as it drops faster and faster. Gareth is helpless. This is going to hurt.

The elevator has only dropped for about five seconds, although it seems like an eternity to Gareth, before an emergency brake cuts in and the elevator starts to slow again. It's just enough to save Gareth's life.

The impact is still bone-jarring and the wheelchair,

sprung in the same way as a car with proper shock absorbers, compresses on its suspension and then recoils upwards like a stunt-car hitting the ramp after jumping a line of buses. Gareth remembers he saw exactly that stunt when he was little and it suddenly pops in to his mind as he is launched up.

He comes out of the seat vertically and then falls back. The wheelchair tilts on two wheels and almost teeters over on its side for one heart-stopping moment before it crunches against the side of the elevator car at a crazy angle and comes to a halt.

Gareth tries to take stock of what has just happened. It is hard to work it out as he is in complete darkness apart from the bright pencil beams of light from the LED headlights built into the end of his arm rests.

He realises he is trapped.

His inert body is half out of the contoured seat. Luckily his eye is still close enough to the Perspex sensor to see the information projected on to it. His one mobile finger can still feel the miniature joystick he uses for moving around the Perspex virtual screen to select options.

Apart from the wheelchair lights he is unable to make out anything in his environment. Panic grips Gareth with a powerful hand and squeezes the breath from his already-compressed lungs. He can feel his heart as it pounds in his constricted chest.

I'm going to die, he thinks with resignation. Squashed like a fly in the corner of a stupid elevator. Alone. My life is about to end.

Gareth has never felt so helpless or so alone. The others don't even know about the elevator shaft under the stairs. They won't know where to look for his body.

The mobile phone built into the wheelchair is useless as there's no signal anywhere. Definitely not 100 feet underground. His mind races as he searches desperately for a potential solution but with so much panic and fear raging through his immobile body he is incapable of rational thought.

I am such an idiot for being curious. What was I thinking? And now I am stuck down a hole like a donkey in a well. A paralysed donkey, that's what I am. To his astonishment he slowly realises that the rasping noise is his own laughter. Hearing a sound, any sound, even his own insane synthesised cackling, calms him slightly.

Enough to start thinking more rationally about his predicament. I'm still in my seat. I have power but I don't know if the wheels were damaged or smashed completely in the impact. What if I try to move and it collapses? I'll die from cold or starvation lying on the floor.

I don't want to die. I want to live.

Gareth moves his finger and selects reverse. He tries moving the wheels a tiny increment and his wheelchair immediately slips an inch or so down the wire mesh of the side of the cage. He stops and waits. Nothing, apart from his own laboured breathing. He can't remember breathing this hard ever. His chest feels like it's going to explode. OK if back doesn't work, maybe forward will. At least the chair is still functioning.

He tries a little forward motion. The wheels slip and then buck slightly against the wire. They grip and the wheelchair regains the tiny amount of height it lost in reverse but won't budge any further. Gareth stops trying and attempts to think of an alternative. But there isn't one. His choices are forwards or backwards.

"Someone help me," he screams in his head although it comes out automated and expressionless through the voice synthesiser.

"Help. Goddamit why can't you hear me. Dad, Rachel. Mum. Someone help me."

"I can't help you darling."

A woman's voice just spoke behind Gareth's head. He experiences a cold terror which instantly replaces the agitation he was feeling a second earlier. Somehow the voice is familiar, but he's not sure why.

"Rachel, is that you?"

Gareth's eyes swivel in their sockets as he tries to see who the voice belongs to you.

"Who's there? Can you get me out of here?"

Terrified, Gareth jerks his wheelchair forwards then backwards timidly, then increasingly violently as his frustration grows. Eventually he applies all the power the chair has got and although it has a top speed of only 5 mph, it is designed to shift a lot of weight so it can push hard, and it leaps forward and away from the wire.

It shoots ahead on two wheels and then slumps back onto all four. Gareth is an expert at manoeuvring his wheelchair and he lurches straight out of the open safety barrier which bounced up when he hit the bottom of the shaft. Gareth does a wild 360 degree spin to locate the source of the voice which just spoke to him, but there is nobody there.

He stops his crazy pirouette on the squealing rubber wheels and takes stock of his environment. He is in an anonymous corridor. The walls and floor are the same bland grey colour. The floor is a shiny painted texture and the walls are bluff breeze blocks. There is what looks like an open door at the end of the long corridor. What the hell is this? he thinks. His natural overriding curiosity is vacuuming all reason from his head once again.

Gareth starts to move down the corridor then stops. I have almost been killed by a mental elevator, there is a power cut, I have no idea where I am and whatever it is I can be pretty certain it is not good. I have to get the others, Gareth realises finally.

He rotates the chair again and whirrs back into the freight elevator. He looks around for the call button and finds it in the focussed beam of the lights. He depresses it with the rubber tip of the probe built into the arm, but nothing happens. The ride down was obviously a one-off.

Gareth backs out of the elevator and hesitates while he weighs up his choices.

"Well, at least I tried to do the sensible thing. Maybe there's another way out."

He says the words out loud without realising he is talking to himself.

Gareth moves forward along the grey corridor into the blackness.

"As if."

The wheelchair casts a circular pool of light around him as he moves down the blackness. Suddenly, the wheels bump over an unseen obstruction. Gareth rotates the wheelchair so he is pointing back the way he came and he swivels the lights down to see what he just hit.

A rat maybe?

As the lights tilt down they pick out a pair of pale, glassy eyes in a round shiny face.

The body of a dead man in US army uniform is wedged up against the wall with one arm stretched across the floor, which explains what he ran over in the dark. Gareth naturally reacts as anyone would and lurches backwards in shock, crashing into the wall as he does so.

He squeals round and heads away from the body as fast as he can. Once through the door Gareth sees another one—open this time—leading to a room which is immersed in blackness. He turns right smartly and rolls into the room.

In the pencil beams of the lights he can see he is in some sort of security control room or maybe even a TV studio. There are dozens of screens on the wall and a desk covered with knobs, buttons and levers. There are six swivel chairs scattered around, some pushed over, one broken.

At the back of the room are two rows of uncomfortable-looking bench seats which would be able to take twelve people. So enough room for eighteen in total. I wonder if they are all dead too? Gareth can't stop the thought forming in his head or the fear which begins to rise in his chest again.

Then he notices a video camcorder which has been left on the long row of coloured plastic buttons of the video desk. It looks a bit scorched and beaten-up. The viewing screen is open. Although it has a crack in the screen it might work, thinks Gareth. He gets close enough to reach it with the extendable titanium probe and tries to hit the play button.

At first all he does is push the camera around a bit and it almost falls on its side. Gareth is intrigued by the camera and feels instinctively that there is something in its memory he needs to watch. A little more trial and error and he strikes lucky. The camera comes to life.

The screen shows some sort of cell or interview room. A man is chained to a chair and he is lurching around violently as if he is trying to escape but the chair appears to be attached to the floor which prevents him from moving too much. Gareth hears a door open and close on the video and the man is suddenly very still.

He is looking around as if he is trying to see what opened the door. Suddenly his chains go tight and he is jerked upright by something. Although obvious the thing is extraordinarily powerful, Gareth can't see it. Whatever "it" is. The man starts to scream but the scream is choked off and he makes a gurgling sound instead as if he is being strangled. There is a low, growling sound like a wild animal. Then the choking and the growling stop at the same instant and the man slumps down. The chains go slack.

He is dead.

A few seconds later there is the sound of the door scraping open again out of vision and two men in US army uniform rush in and go to the man. They unchain him and lift him out of the chair. They are calling for a medic.

Then there is another deep, unearthly, satanic growl from somewhere in the room or outside. To his horror, Gareth realises the sound may not have been on the camera this time. His eyes bulge in fear and he hits the off button on the video camera.

It is suddenly very dark and still in the room.

Gareth listens. There is silence. Maybe he was mistaken. Then there it is again. It's not until it actually happens to you personally do you understand what it means when someone describes the hairs on the back of their neck standing up. His neck prickles.

Gareth hooks the camera with the probe and reverses out of the room as fast as possible and heads back the way he came. And the growling is there again behind him. Louder and angrier.

Gareth almost rolls the wheelchair on its side again in his panic to escape whatever is chasing him. He finds his way back to the elevator entrance and skids round into the elevator backwards with the headlights shining out into the darkness. The lights pick out the door at the end of the corridor where he has just been. Someone has closed it. The dead guy is still where he lay before.

Gareth's eyes are the only way he can register emotion which they do in spades as the door starts to open very slowly. There is a low groaning growl which sounds almost sleepy though still very menacing. The door opens wider and into the bright, white beam of the wheelchair headlights comes Ted.

"Ted what the hell are you doing here?" grates Gareth.

"I could ask you the same question," replies Ted. "How did you get down here?"

"I sort of fell by accident. It's good to see you. How about you?" replies Gareth, backing further into the elevator.

"I abseiled down the shaft. I woke up as I thought I heard your voice. It was you wasn't it?" asks Ted.

"I was yelling like crazy. I got stuck. I was scared I was going to die. No one knows about this place."

"You OK?"

"Shit scared and sore. Can we go?"

"Well no. There's no power, remember? We'll have to work out how to winch you back up or something."

"I don't care. I just want to get out of here. Some weird shit happened."

"I bet. OK. Give me five minutes. I'm going to see what else I can find."

"No Ted. Wait! I..."

But Ted has vanished before Gareth can warn him about what he's just discovered. Gareth waits in the relative safety of the elevator where the only angle anything can attack him is from the front in the glare of the beams.

He waits for Ted to come back in the stillness. In a way Ted suddenly appearing then going again has heightened Gareth's sense of isolation and fear. All at once Gareth realises how very tired he is. A bone tired which he can't remember ever experiencing. Must be fear and adrenaline.

More time passes and Ted still doesn't reappear. Oh God, thinks Gareth. Has it got him too? Whatever it is.

Gareth's headlights start to dim. They fade slowly and then go out altogether. The only illumination is the green glow from the Perspex eye reticule in front of Gareth's face but that too starts to fade until it blinks out. Gareth is sitting in pitch black listening to the sound of his own breathing

"Gareth?"

It's a woman's voice.

"Who's there?" Gareth's voice synthesiser continues to function on a separate emergency power supply.

"Gareth, it's your mother."

A soft, warm brown voice. A woman's voice.

Blackness.

"I'm with Greg. He wants to say hello."

"Is this a trick?" is all Gareth can manage as everything he has been clinging onto evaporates altogether.

"Your twin Greg. You remember him don't you darling? He's the one who killed me, not you. He shot me in the back with your daddy's gun."

Gareth is crying in the dark or, rather, his version of

crying. Locked In Syndrome prevents him from registering proper physiological reactions but he can cry with his voice. But the sound which comes out is more like a long stuttering sniffle.

"Are you...are you Delissa?"

"Yes dear. That's right. It's me. You don't really remember me. You were too young but you remember my voice don't you? Every boy knows his mother's voice."

"I remember."

"To make amends for what your brother did to me Gareth, you must all die too." The soft female voice suddenly becomes demonic and harsh.

"All of you!" it bellows deafeningly in a sudden chorus of male voices straight out of the depths of hell.

Then there is silence. Gareth's heart is pounding in his ears and he feels like his head will explode. His breathing is harsh and erratic. And still the blackness. He can feel himself slipping deeper and deeper into himself. He wonders if he is dying now. Blackness fills his mind as well as his eyes. The sound of his own breathing fades to nothing.

Gareth is standing at the top of a flight of stairs. He is holding a shotgun unsteadily. It feels massive in his puny hands. Gareth looks about ten years old. A woman is clinging to the banister rail. Her hands are white and bony. The woman is looking deep into his eyes. She is very agitated and scared.

"Greg please put your father's gun down. It could be loaded," she pleads.

He recognises the voice from the darkness.

"Why do you keep calling me Greg? My name is

Gareth. Greg is my twin," Gareth replies.

"No darling you are Greg. Gareth doesn't exist. That's what the doctor told you remember darling?"

"Why do you make daddy cry every night?"

"It's not me, darling. He is very unhappy. Because of what happened in that helicopter and afterwards. It wasn't anyone's fault Greg. Not his, not mine, not yours. Please put the gun down you are really frightening me."

"I can stand," Gareth observes simply. He looks down in confusion and astonishment at his body.

"Of course you can darling. But you are a big boy and I'm scared you are going to hurt me."

"I'm not going to."

"That's a relief."

"But Greg might."

There is a startling bang and a blinding flash. Gareth is in darkness once again. There is no light and the only thing he can hear is his own laboured breathing.

Suddenly there is light and a face is inches from his. His eyes, the only instrument Gareth has for expressing emotion, widen and stay wide. Ted is leaning down, his hands on his knees. The power is back. A look of concern turns to amusement as Ted shrugs back the loop of mountaineering rope coiled round his meaty shoulder.

"Christ. You look like that dude Alex in A Clockwork Orange when they're brainwashing him and they force his eyes open with clamps and make him watch porn while they feed him drugs to make him nauseous and shit."

Gareth says very slowly and uncertainly, "I...don't remember that movie."

Gareth is still parked in the entrance to the freight elevator and with the resumption of the power supply recessed greenish neon transforms the terrifying dungeon into the safe, neutral atmosphere of a hospital.

"And we have power. I'm telling you dude. This place is cracked."

Ted pushes Gareth backwards gently into the elevator and slides the gate down.

"What have you got there Cochise? A camera?"

Ted stabs the call button and the elevator jerks hard once as it winds in the slack from the emergency stop then it starts to hum upwards.

"Where would we be without electricity?"

"At the bottom of a fucking lift shaft," grates the voice synthesiser.

"You need a power boost dude? That why you were sitting there in the dark?" asks Ted cheerily.

"Yes. My voice synthesiser is the only bit still working."

"Who were you talking to?"

"I wasn't talking to anyone."

"I could hear your voice and some woman I didn't recognise."

"You were imagining it."

After the confusing things the ghost, demon or hallucination—whatever it was—have just told him, Gareth is no longer in the mood to discuss it.

# Video diary

Dawn has broken and the atmosphere in the castle has lifted with the dawn mist to be replaced by a much more normal mood. Darkness has a way of sucking the life out of you where each breath becomes an effort, Gareth is thinking to himself. He is plugged into a socket next to a charger someone has found for the camera.

All six of the climbing party are gathered round the island in the kitchen. They lean in under the central light. Their faces are illuminated by the warm glow of the light.

It's like last night never happened, muses Gareth.

"So Gareth has got something for us to watch after he fell down a hole and almost broke his neck. Against my specific orders to stay in the main hall and not start trundling around the place. I knew I should have slept downstairs and kept an eye on you." Trent looks at Gareth and runs his hands through his greying hair in frustration.

"I was bored," counters Gareth.

"And almost dead," adds Rachel.

Robin hugs Gareth. He scrunches up his eyes in disgust.

"OK, thanks but no touching. I've been through enough without that as well," he says through the synthesiser.

Rula kicks the tyre of his wheelchair.

"We're just glad you're OK. We're in enough shit already and a death could really put a downer on the holiday."

Eli is wearing a serious expression. He leans against the breakfast island with his back to Trent.

"Seriously man. You could have got into a whole bunch more trouble in a situation like that. As we used to say in the Airborne, don't go forward if there's no way back. Your old man won't say it being all fucked up and all but that can't have been funny."

Trent smacks his hand on the wooden surface angrily. "Hey Eli. You're not the guy's father. Stay out of this."

Eli turns in to face Trent. "You could be a little more simpatico. The kid has no way of defending himself. That should be your job."

Ted steps in between the outbreak of testosterone and gently but firmly pushes the two men apart with his huge hands.

"I think we should have a look at what's on that camera. I have a feeling it ain't pretty."

Ted presses the play button as they huddle round the tiny broken screen. The image of the man in chains, which Gareth watched in the basement, starts to replay. Gareth studies their reaction to the terrified screams of the man, his choking death rattle and the other men rushing in to try and save him when he has clearly been killed by an unseen force.

Trent is impassive. Eli is twirling his hunting knife on its tip on the wooden breakfast island. Rachel has her hand over her mouth in horror and it occurs to Gareth the women look like the three monkeys. Robin has her hands over her ears and Rula is covering her eyes by the end of the man's screaming. Ted has his huge arms folded and is leaning in, fascinated.

Then there is the demonic, deeply evil growling Gareth heard but it's on the tape too. Did he imagine he heard it for real? He is no longer sure. He's no longer sure of anything he realises.

The clip finishes and there is static. Trent hits the off button, but not before a shot of a blonde man appears in what looks like an interrogation room. He starts to speak but is gone as the screen goes blank. Trent is holding his hand over the camera as if he is willing what they just saw to go away. To never have existed. Now they all have what they just saw on the camera in their reality for good.

"That was some weird shit," Ted says to break the spell.

Silence.

"The question is what should we do about it?" asks Trent in a slow deliberate voice.

"We have to go to the authorities with it. And soon," exclaims Rachel.

Rula grabs the camera. "We need to leave right now. Gareth must be able to get a couple of miles before his battery goes flat and then we can take it in turns to carry him. It's the only option."

Eli stops spinning the knife on its tip, grabs the handle and flips it a couple of times then deftly replaces it in the sheath strapped to his thigh.

"Why bother? Someone is gonna get their ass up here today sometime to deliver mail or come to check on whoever was here until we rocked up. I vote we chill and wait for rescue."

Robin snaps out of her trance. "I can't believe we are discussing options. We just watched someone murdered by an invisible...thing. It's going to get us all too if we stay here a minute longer. I'll fight anyone I can see but not this. We have to go."

Another argument erupts in one instant as panic ripples through all of them. The raised, angry, scared voices rise in pitch and fury. In particular the tension between Trent and Eli, the two alpha males, bursts out and they are almost at blows. Eye to eye and facing off like a couple of buffalo in a turf war. The noise is deafening as the tension and anxiety from the previous twenty four hours surfaces.

"There's more."

Gareth's strange synthesised voice somehow cuts through the fight and there is suddenly silence. Heads turn and they look at the expressionless still form in the wheelchair.

"Say what?" asks Eli.

"On the camera. There was another guy. I saw it."

Gareth stares back at them then his eyes go to the battered and scorched VCR. "It might give us some answers."

"No way. Period."

Trent puts his hand protectively over the camera.

"What have we got to lose Trent? It can't get any weirder than the clip we just saw. Maybe there is something which will solve this shit storm?" Ted sits back in his bar stool and fixes Trent with a rebellious stare.

"Other...things happened down there dad. I think we should watch the rest of it."

The emotion in Gareth's synthesised voice is in total contrast to his impassive, paralysed face.

Trent looks around at his wife and friends. They return his glare with a resolute expression.

"Play the video, Trent. It can't be any worse."

Rachel puts her arm around Rula's shoulders as she is starting to shake. Ted slips his hand into Rula's and gives it a squeeze. She smiles bravely at him although the shaking doesn't subside.

"Goddamit."

Trent hits play.

The VCR screen blinks and flashes twice then the image Gareth glimpsed appears. A handsome man wearing a black crew-neck woollen jumper is seated at a metal table identical to which the murdered man was chained. He has bright white blonde hair which is shoulder length. It is thick and wavy. He has the aura of authority and money.

Calm and at ease, the man is looking at a single point behind the camera. A little time passes then an unseen person clears their throat.

"Well are we going to sit here all day and admire each other or are you going to tell me what I need to know?" asks the anonymous voice. It belongs to an American and someone used to being in control. The voice is relaxed and friendly. Unhurried. This guy has all the time in the world.

"You mean am I terrorist?" asks the blonde man.

"That would be a good place to start," replies the voice.

"Do I look like a terrorist?"

The blonde man smiles disarmingly, shrugs and sits back in his chair. It appears to be bolted to the floor as it doesn't move a molecule. The blonde man lounges with one leg extended and the other bent as he stretches a chained arm along the back rest of the chair. He places his left arm on the surface of the metal table with his palm up in a gesture of resignation.

"Never quite know what a terrorist is supposed to

look like," comes the reply.

"Oh you know, scarf wrapped around the head, big bushy beard, sunglasses, AK-47 slung across my back. Waistcoat made of plastic explosive," teases the blonde man.

"You were found inside the compound fence by our patrol with your associates. How did you get there and what were you planning to do?" asks the voice, more insistently this time.

The blonde man leans down and looks at the floor. He rests his elbows on his knees and puts his head in his hands. He takes a deep breath and sits up again as if he has just decided something. He runs both hands though his thick blonde hair and pushes it backwards until the chains interrupt the motion with a stubborn clank. For the first time, his freakishly deep blue eyes bore into his unseen interrogator.

"We came to warn you."

"Warn us about what?" asks the voice.

"You are playing with a power you don't understand," replies the blonde man deliberately but with a sudden chill in his tone. His friendly, relaxed demeanour has gone.

"What we're doing here is classified. Are you a spy? Who are you working for?" asks the voice, annoyed now.

"I think I should tell you a story," says the blonde man softly.

"If you have to. I've got all day so knock yourself out," replies the voice, changing tack.

In an even voice, the blonde man tells his interrogator a crazy-sounding story of how hundreds of thousands of years ago some of God's angels decided they wanted to experience what it was like to be human, spurred on by an archangel called Lucifer. This caused a rift between God and the ringleader Lucifer.

He talks about a battle between the warring factions of Lucifer and the Archangels Michael, Uriel and Gabriel. Lucifer and his rebellious followers are defeated by the supremely powerful archangels and thrown into a pit where they are prevented from achieving their goal of becoming human. But compassionate Archangel Gabriel feels pity for them and throws his lyre—a harp—into the cave to lift their spirits.

The lyre plays the music of angels and is a powerful magical instrument.

"This guy is whack," grunts Ted.

But the others, captivated by the story, gesture for Ted to keep quiet.

"I have to know how where this is going," chirps Gareth.

"If that guy is out to harm anyone, I'll eat Gareth's orthopaedic cushion," laughs Rula.

The blonde man is in the zone now and nothing is going to stop him finishing his tale.

"You see, this is where the Ark of the Covenant, the most holy of God's gifts to his children, derived its power. From Gabriel's magic lyre. The lyre was said to be one of the objects hidden in the ark along with the staff of St Germaine and later the shroud Jesus was wrapped in when he was brought down from the cross.

"The ancient people, the Hittites, used the ark as a weapon against the Pharisees in what is now known as Egypt. The Pharisees coveted the power of the ark and eventually captured it. But it brought them so much bad luck they believed with floods and pestilence that they gave it back and it was thought to have ended up in the hands of the Jews—the descendants of the Pharisees—

in the Temple of King David on the Mount in Jerusalem.

"The fallen angels and their leader Lucifer or Satan as he became to be known, having spent millennia in the cave, escaped and they became the Watchers, earthbound angels who walk amongst men still today but are now known as the Nephilim. They are attracted to powerful regimes and powerful people and are not always...good.

"Satan was the most evil of the fallen angels. He separated from the Watchers and he became God's nemesis. His arch enemy.

"It is believed," the blond man says, "that Satan is still trapped in the cave and can only walk the planet at night. When you hear him playing beautiful music on Gabriel's lyre it is to lure people to join him in hell.

"Where is the ark? Is it possible to weaponise it if we found it?" asks the interrogator eagerly.

"You're not listening to a word I'm saying are you Gates?" The blonde man sighs. "Yes. Closer than you think and yes... it is the deadliest weapon in the universe."

"So is that why you came here?" asks the interrogator Gates slowly.

"No, it was to give you this warning. If you continue with this interference in forces you don't understand, you will destroy yourselves like the Pharisee by tapping into powers you cannot control once you release them," states the blonde main calmly.

"Destroy ourselves? So that doesn't include you?" asks Gates.

"No."

"And why is that?"

"Ah, that is the part I can't explain." The blonde

man smiles and sits back, somehow satisfied with the conversation.

Rachel presses the button on the battered little camera and the image dies.

"That music we heard..." her voice trails off.

"Okayyy, did everyone get that? The angels have landed and we have got ourselves caught in the middle of a conspiracy to steal nukes or something. Makes Apache folklore sound sensible." Ted guffaws.

"Wait a minute, just wait a minute." Robin holds up her hands.

"Here we go," snorts Rula. "Our middle east correspondent speaks."

"Take your mouth out of transmit for just one second, Rula. You might learn something." Robin kneels on a breakfast bar stool to purchase a little more height so everyone will hear her.

"Historically that guy was spot on."

"Well, that's a matter of opinion," retorts Rula. "The ark was supposed to have been used by Joshua to attack Jericho and flatten its walls but according to archaeologists that never happened. And neither did lots of other stuff. Particularly in the Old Testament."

"Unbelievable—are you denying a Jewish attack took place on my ancestors, the Philistines?" Robin looks really shocked.

"What? No of course not. Actually I don't know. None of us do for sure. I'm just saying all this history is so uncertain—never mind some crazy theory about angels and demons," stutters Rula, feeling defensive.

"I can't believe we're debating the Old Testament when we've just been watching a man in the here and now being murdered by an invisible something or other. A something which could do the same to us," says

Rachel flatly.

Eli has been watching this spat and steps in.

"I'm no expert at history, religion or who has the right to what but my favourite book when I was a kid growing up in Mexico was the Book of Enoch."

"What's that?" asks Rula, genuinely interested.

"It was a book in the Bible like the Book of Genesis but it was kicked out by the Roman Catholics," he replies, almost apologetically. "It may have never have even been in the Bible in the first place. What was really cool about it was your faith, Rula, was based on it. Enoch was supposed to be the same guy as the prophet Elijah in the Talmud, your holy book."

"And?" asks Trent impatiently. "What has it got to do with this?"

"That dude was on the money with what he said. That's how it was told in the Book of Enoch. It was all about the battle between the good and bad angels and the lyre and all." Eli says.

"OK, enough talk. Time to do," Trent snaps impatiently. "I suggest Ted and Eli try to walk out of here and scare up some help. That alright with you guys?"

Ted and Eli nod. They must weigh 500 pounds between them. Robin steps forward.

"Can I go too? I'm the fittest person here. It's not all about size you know."

Trent looks at Robin, weighing up the question.

"And since when were you my dad?" Robin fires the question at Trent as he is about to speak. Instead he raises his hands and shrugs.

"Better," smiles Robin. Ted, Eli and Robin prepare to leave.

An hour later Ted, Eli and Robin are walking at an easy pace across the moorland away from the castle. The morning sun warms their backs. Purple heather lies underfoot with tiny bright yellow flowers which have bloomed in the summer sun. To follow the winding road down the Cairngorm mountainside would take far too long.

The drive up had taken an hour so they have decided to walk the route as the crow flies—straight. They crisscross the road again and again. They are making good progress. They will be amongst civilisation before it gets dark for sure.

They walk on at a brisk pace in silence. All of them are carrying a back pack. They are glad to be doing something active and enjoying some fresh air at last.

Two crows wheel around above them. They caw to each other as they ride the air current moving up the incline of the mountain. As the terrain changes Ted, Eli and Robin enter a deep gulley which seems to have a natural path winding through the chasm between the slabs of rock on either side. The crows spinning and diving above them change direction and glide away down the gulley. They disappear and are finally silent.

"At last," Ted says as he adjusts his pack. "Noisy little bastards."

Protected from the cold wind which draws across the highlands permanently in the gulley, it is suddenly still and silent.

Eli cocks his handsome South American native Indian head to one side and stops.

"Can you hear that?" he asks.

"What?" replies Robin. "I can't hear anything."

"That's just it," grins Eli. "Not a sound. Beautiful."

They walk on with their heavy footfalls the only

sound which echoes up the sides of the gulley. Then there is a growl.

"Is that what I think it was?" asks Ted incredulously.

They have frozen in mid-step.

"That came from in front of us," states Robin. "What is it?"

"It sounded like a big mountain cat like a cougar. Does Scotland have cougars?" whispers Eli.

"Not last time I checked," Ted whispers back. Eli draws his hunting knife and motions the other two to wait.

"Eli!" hisses Ted but Eli is gone.

"Oh for the love of the great leader Cochise. Can you stay here Robin? I'm going to track round and track that thing. I feel it came from behind like you. I want to make sure it's not following us."

And with that, Ted slopes off on silent steps like the Apache tracker he is at heart, leaving Robin standing resolutely in the middle of the gulley, alone.

Despite herself, Robin is scared and finds she is hyperventilating. She shrugs off her pack and slides a small metal pan out of its tether. She grips it with both hands and shifts her weight from foot to foot as she rotates repeatedly, ready to fight if necessary. Sweat trickles down her brow and she wipes it away with the back of her hand.

There is another growl, closer this time. She can't tell where it's coming from which increases her rate of rotation. After what seems like an age but in fact is only thirty seconds, Ted comes back into view. He shrugs and smiles.

Then the sound of Eli screaming in a mix of terror and rage bounces off the walls of the gulley. They run toward the sound to find Eli lying on the ground. His hunting knife is sticking out of a wound on his left side just above the waist and he is covered with slashes which are bleeding badly.

"I couldn't... see it..." he whispers between gasps for breath.

Ted and Robin are so horrified by the viciousness of Eli's wounds they are paralysed for a split second then they both snap into survival mode. Robin squats down on her haunches next to Eli and speaks into his ear.

"Don't talk we need to get this sorted."

She turns to look at Ted who is running his hands over Eli's limbs checking for broken bones.

She addresses Ted so Eli can't hear her.

"Has it gone?"

Ted is checking the artery in Eli's neck for his pulse.

"How would I know? He says he couldn't see it. Maybe it's still here. I feel like it's gone through my hair. We need to make a decision and quickly."

"What? Whether to leave him here?" she shoots back. "Your hair?"

"Long story. No for Chrissakes—we're going to have to get him back up to the castle before darkness falls. If we see a vehicle we'll get them to stop but I wouldn't hold your breath. This place has turned into the moon. Really strange. No I mean do we leave the knife in or take it out?"

"It might do enough damage to kill him if we do. The other cuts aren't deep, just messy." Robin touches the hilt of the hunting knife projecting from Eli's muscular, fat free torso. Eli flinches.

"Let's take it out. Eli—should I take the knife out?" Ted directs the question to Eli.

"Take it out dude. No way am I walking back to the castle with that thing in my side grinding away."

Eli glances down at the knife and grimaces.

Ted looks at Robin and then kneels down next to his friend and slips his fingers either side of the blade to compress the flesh to hold it in place when he pulls it out. Ted gazes into Eli's eyes and makes sure he has his attention.

"OK dude. On three. One, two -,"He slides the big knife out.

"Ahh shit! That hurts. You said on three," grunts Eli.

"I lied. I didn't want you to tense. You alright?" smiles Ted.

Blood starts to flow from the stab wound. Robin wipes away the blood and splashes some water into the wound from her tin bottle. Then she unscrews the cap from a tiny tube and squirts some clear liquid on the mouth of the cut which is an inch and a half wide. She squeezes both sides together and waits for a few seconds. Satisfied, she unwraps a compression bandage and straps Eli's waist up with her scarf.

"There, that should stop you bleeding to death before we get you back," she says sounding more confident than she feels.

They haul Eli to his feet. As they start to lurchingly retrace their steps back up the gulley, Ted asks, "What was that stuff?"

Robin looks at him.

"Superglue," she replies matter of factly.

# Into The Basement

Night is falling again at the castle. Trent, Gareth, Rachel and Rula are relaxing in the kitchen. They are grouped around the breakfast island and haven't really moved since the others left in the morning.

Gareth is amusing himself by doing wheelies up and down the kitchen.

Trent is trying to ignore him but snaps and asks him to stop. Gareth whirrs over to Rachel. She looks up and smiles warmly at him.

"Hey what's up?" she asks.

Gareth sits motionless in the Recaro seat and stares at her without blinking.

"Gareth, it makes me a little uncomfortable when you do that. I can't tell what you're thinking. Just so you know you look like you want to kill me."

Gareth continues to stare at Rachel.

"Looking happy is a bit of challenge for me Rachel. I'm laughing inside though. Listen. Ha ha ha."

"Gareth please. You know what I mean. I think you forget how unnerving being stared at is." She holds herself without realising.

"Can I talk to you?" Gareth asks.

He draws even closer. Rachel studies his face for any sign of an emotional clue but there is no trace as always. There never will be she thinks sadly. She nods.

"Sure you know you can. Any time. Shall we go

somewhere we can talk?"

In the library, Gareth wheels as close to Rachel as he can. The defensive look on Rachel's face shows she is expecting some sort of showdown.

"Well? What is on your mind Gareth? Let's have it."

Gareth is silent. He fidgets with the position of the wheelchair which is his way of playing for time while he thinks. He knows how uncomfortable it makes others when he does nothing except stare if he doesn't know what to say. He can't exactly pace up and down in front of the fireplace. He can't do anything, even if his mind is spinning. It's that which he really hates about his condition, although he's had it for half his life now and can't remember being any other way.

But it's that memory of his childhood which has just been dragged suddenly to the surface by his terrifying experience in the bizarre hell hole which is bothering him so profoundly.

"I want to talk about what happened in the basement," he says finally.

"OK good. I thought you might tell me about it eventually. Take your time," soothes Rachel,

"Don't get all therapist on me Rachel. I need to talk to you as my mom," retorts Gareth in the same flat emotionless tone his synthesiser delivers everything.

"Sorry. Of course. So what happened exactly? It was more than the shock of the business with the elevator almost killing you wasn't it?"

Rachel puts a hand on Gareth's knee.

"No touching. It makes me uncomfortable."

Rachel withdraws her hand sharply and puts her hands in her lap.

Gareth tells Rachel the whole story, in terse splinters of words from his voice box at first then as he warms up the trickle becomes a torrent.

"Slow down Gareth," Rachel gesticulates for Gareth to throttle back. "Are you saying there was a person down there with you?"

"Not a person, just a voice coming from nowhere. Like it was all around me," he states flatly.

Gareth admits her voice sounded familiar and then when she said she was her mother Delissa he started to pass out or something. He tells Rachel about the dream and the gun.

"She couldn't seem to tell the difference between me and my twin Greg. One of us had dad's gun and was pointing it at her. She was really frightened."

Rachel is very still and says nothing. She is struggling to keep her expression neutral. She is looking into Gareth's eyes and they gaze at each other for what seems like minutes.

"You didn't have a twin Gareth. Greg doesn't...didn't...exist."

"You're lying."

If Gareth could scream this would be the moment but it comes out as a flat, unemotional statement.

Rachel doesn't blink or avert her gaze. Tears start to glisten in the corners of her eyes.

"I'm not Gareth darling. It's the truth. You seemed to invent Greg after your mother, Delissa, died."

"No. Greg was my twin. We were together. I remember him."

"You think you do. But I'm afraid Greg was just a fantasy figure you created after the death. A copy of yourself. To help you cope."

After what seems like an eternity to Rachel, Gareth finally asks the question which is hanging in the room like a bad smell.

"Cope with what? Her dying and leaving us on her own while I turned into...this?"

Rachel tries to smile but the mask slips a little and her chin starts to tremble. I am not going to lose it now, she thinks. I have to be strong. Where's Trent when I need him?

"I think I need to get your father," she says firmly.

"Why? What's the big secret? Tell me," intones Gareth flatly.

The room is plunged into darkness. They sit sound-lessly while their eyes adjust to the sudden blackness.

"If that isn't a sign..." says Rachel into the gloom.

"What is it with this place and night time?" asks Rachel more to herself than Gareth.

Eli is spread-eagled across the kitchen breakfast is-land in the centre of the room. The field dressing above his waist is soaked red and blood from the other cuts has turned his cream and grey hiking clothes almost a uniform crimson.

Trent, Ted and Robin work frantically around him as they wind up a charge into the field lights and search for something they can use to dress the wounds. Eli is pale under his deep tan. His lips are turning blue and his eyes roll around in their sockets as he slips in and out of unconsciousness.

Robin and Ted are both covered in Eli's blood from half-carrying, half-dragging the Mexican ex-Navy Seal across two miles of damp heather. They are ex-hausted and semi-circles of tiredness are etched under both their eyes. They work silently with Trent on the stab wound and the myriad of slash marks which have ripped through the light cotton of Eli's clothes.

Robin has found a head torch and is examining the dozen or so slashes with a more scrupulous gaze.

"As if we didn't have enough problems," she mutters under her breath. Trent catches the words and looks at her quizzically.

She answers his look.

"The cuts are only a couple of hours old but some of them are showing signs of infection already. That isn't possible."

"Eli needs proper medical attention and fast," agrees Trent.

Robin looks at some of the cuts more closely.

"He's gonna get septicaemia first then go into shock... then die. He needs morphine, antibiotics and a transfusion. I don't think he'll last the night."

"We can't let that happen. Any suggestions?" asks Trent.

It's the first time he's invited an opinion from anyone else he's actually meant. Robin studies Trent while she weighs up the options. For the first time she notices how much Trent's hands are shaking.

"Are you OK?" whispers Robin.

"Eli was with us in Afghanistan. We were carrying some of his unit in the Chinook the night we got taken out by the Taliban RPG. He stayed back at base as it wasn't his turn to go out on a mission. He was the guy who got me out of the wreckage. The Taliban were less than 100 yards away from us when he got there in another chopper. He and his boys saved us from being captured and certain death. I owe him. We can't just let him die."

"No we can't. There must be a way of getting help," agrees Robin.

Ted has been listening and steps in.

"If you're looking for suggestions I have one but you're not going to like it."

"Which is?" asks Trent gently.

"The solution may lie down below."

Ted alternates his gaze between Trent and Robin to read their reaction. Trent looks at both of them and then down at Eli, who is obviously slipping away.

"OK, we go. But just the three of us. Rachel and Rula will have to stay up here with Gareth and keep an eye on Eli."

Robin is bent over Eli and is studying something on the end of a kitchen knife. She moves closer to a light and inspects the tip of the blade.

"How strange. There are what look like fish scales in the wounds. Wait, scratch that, more like snake skin."

Ted squints at the glistening sliver on the tip of Robin's knife and shakes his gigantic head.

"What the fuck are we up against? A fucking reptile?" he asks of no one in particular.

Trent picks up Eli's hunting knife in its sheath and stares at it, thinking.

"Whatever it is I think we are going to have to kill it before we are able to leave this castle."

Trent wraps Eli's hunting knife in its sheath around his right leg and tightens it with an air of finality.

With the elevator out of action from the power cut, they decide to abseil down the shaft. They are at the mouth of the elevator coiling ropes and checking their caribiners when Rachel and Rula come round the corner.

"And where do you think you are you going?" asks Rachel archly.

"To see if there is such a thing as an emergency room down there," offers Ted.

"After what Gareth went through? I don't think so." Rachel's voice is flat and uncompromising. "And why are you climbing down anyway? Why not use the elevator again?"

Trent interrupts. "Power? Cut? Gareth in a pile? Ring any bells?"

"He got it to work when the power was off. Have you even tried Trent?" Rachel replies sharply.

Ted steps between the warring couple.

"Whoa, whoa. Time out. Trent—try to let other people speak. Rachel—no we haven't but there's no way we want to end up a few feet shorter at the bottom of the shaft. That thing seems to have a mind of its own."

Rula grabs a rope and starts sliding caribiners onto her waist harness which she lifts off the floor and buckles around her hips.

"And where do you think you're going?" asks Rachel, hands on hips.

"I'm sick of being a reaction. I want to be an action," Rula states simply.

"What I object to is no one consulted me first." Rachel addresses the criticism to her husband Trent.

"You weren't here and there's no time. It was Ted's idea anyway not mine," replies Trent.

"So that makes it OK?" asks Rachel, bridling at being undermined.

"Didn't you say I needed to let others make decisions for themselves and to stop being a control freak?" teases Trent.

"Sod it. If you're all going, I'm coming too." Rachel is wriggling into her climbing gear too.

"What about Eli?" asks Robin.

Gareth whirrs into view from the kitchen.

"Leave me a walkie talkie. I can talk to you on that."

"Exactly how are you going to do that?" asks Robin.

Gareth extends his titanium probe and wiggles it up and down.

"Plug the headset into my external RF jack. I'll be able to hear you and if I need to speak the chair software will take care of it."

"If you say so, dude. Here." Ted connects a walkie talkie to Gareth's headset jack and slides the handset into one of the slots on the side of the high-tech wheelchair.

Ted raises another walkie talkie and presses the "Speak" button.

"Hello Cochise. Hel-."

A shriek of feedback howls round the hall.

"Um, maybe I should stand further away?" Ted suggests sheepishly.

Gareth disappears with the walkie talkie round a corner. Ted's unit crackles into life.

"Hey Ted, can you hear me?"

Ted hits transmit.

"Loud and clear buddy. Loud and clear."

Ted slips the walkie into his gilet and moves his bulk over to the elevator shaft. The walkie talkie bursts into life again.

"Hear me now? Ha ha."

Gareth's monotone synthesised voice echoes round the hall once again.

Ted replies, "If you don't stay off this thing Gareth I am going to come and kick your ass. Now cut it out.

We'll be connected the whole time. If there's any change in Eli's condition before we get back let us know. We shouldn't be gone more than fifteen minutes, twenty max. Only talk to me if it's important. Over."

"Roger that," drones Gareth's synthesised voice made extra tinny by the small speaker in the walkie talk-ie.

Ted acts as anchor man for Trent and Robin first as they lower themselves though an inspection hatch in the floor of the freight elevator and they slip away down the shaft. Each climber's rope is looped round the overhead supports of the elevator car in succession. Rachel goes next. Rula is about to lower herself through the hatch when she hesitates.

"You OK?" asks Ted softly.

Rula looks round and their eyes meet. She half smiles and reaches out for his hand which she squeezes.

He squeezes back and steps in slowly to give Rula a hug. She looks up at the gentle giant and her lips part. Ted is bending down to kiss her when Trent interrupts the moment from below.

"Rula are you coming or do we have to hang around here all day waiting for you?"

Rula shrugs and places two fingers on Ted's lips.

"Raincheck?" she asks.

"I'll bring an umbrella," Ted replies, smiling shyly. Then she is gone. Ted loops his own rope round the steel pole and he too disappears.

Gareth has been watching their departure half-hidden in the doorway to the kitchen. Eli is still lying motionless on the wooden breakfast island which is providing a makeshift field hospital. Gareth looks at Eli carefully from both sides. Satisfied he is still breathing, he rotates and heads for where the video camera is sitting on a table.

He presses the play button built into the flip out screen on the side and he watches the end of the clip showing the blonde man being interrogated. Something catches his eye in the background as the blonde man is talking about playing with a power they don't understand. Gareth rewinds the digital file a few seconds and presses play.

There! A shadow seems to move behind the blonde man. He is almost certain. He rewinds and plays the same section again. He hits pause and captures a large black shape moving behind the blonde man which looks like a fuzzy grey snowball. Yes! What is that?

Gareth presses play and the picture breaks up into static again at the point they reached earlier before the conclusion of the interview. It continues to play and there is another clip which distorts and crackles slightly before settling down. It's another interview room, similar to the other one but larger with some sort of mirror half visible behind the heads of the two people sitting chained to a desk, like the man who was choked to death.

One of the captives is a thin man in his mid to late twenties with long, black unruly hair. The other is a slightly overweight woman with a pretty face who looks maybe ten years older than the man. She too has black hair which looks like it hasn't seen a brush for a few weeks. They are dressed in the type of orange suits found in every correctional institute in the US.

"How long have you been in our care now?" asks a disembodied voice. The woman replies first.

"I have no clue. A long time. Difficult to say since you took away my watch and there are no windows down here."

"Makes it easier to contain you," answers the voice. There is a nasty, bullying tone to it.

"Who are you people anyway?" asks the thin man through a curtain of dirty black hair.

"I am Colonel Hassan and you are Rafael, is that correct?" asks the haughty voice belonging to the colonel.

"You know who I am, Hassan. I am your worst nightmare," sneers the thin man.

"Once again, what were you doing in a Defense Department Facility with no authorisation?" asks the cruel-sounding voice.

"Oh can I answer that one? Again. We broke in to find the proof that we need to show the world you are going to destroy our planet with the thing you have built here," replies the dishevelled woman.

"Gabriela—can I call you Gabriela?—This is a high security, Government scientific research facility. You had no business being here and technically you have committed treason. You know when we go to trial you are looking at least 30 years to life wearing those very cute overalls don't you? They should make you a lot of friends in the penitentiary."

The thin man tries to stand but is stopped short half way up by the chains.

"This situation is barbaric. We share the same country and you know all too well that what you're doing to us is illegal, not to mention immoral."

There is a loud and unpleasant laugh from the man who owns the voice.

"Spare me. You have no rights here. You're lucky you're still alive."

Rafaela grunts in disgust.

"Tell that to Julian Assange, Bradley Manning or

Edward Snowden."

Eli groans and shifts his position slightly, making Gareth snap out of the interview for a second. A trickle of blood appears from under Eli's back and snakes its way across the wooden surface until it drips into a puddle on the floor. Gareth whirrs quietly over to him and activates the walkie talkie transmit button.

"Ted, are you there?" Gareth intones in his flat expressionless robotic voice. He waits, his eyes locked on Eli. There is no response.

"Ted? Dad? Can you hear me? Over." Still nothing.

"If you can hear me Eli is bleeding more. I think you should come back. Over."

Gareth is alarmed by Eli's rapidly-deteriorating condition. He has no way of monitoring his vital signs like blood pressure or his heartbeat. He looks godawful. He's going to die, thinks Gareth. I hope it's not my fault. He thinks back to when he was compiling a mental list of who he would kill first and Eli would have been first, right? I wonder if I'm psychic or have some sort of bad energy?

Who said thoughts become things?

I promise from this moment forward I will never, ever have another bad thought about death, killing or any associated activity. It must be twenty minutes since all the others went down the shaft. Maybe it's killed them. I did imagine them all dead on my list and now look at Eli. He's well on the way.

In an attempt to occupy his rapidly-unravelling mind, Gareth goes back to the video camera and picks up where he left off in the paused clip.

"You don't know what you're dealing with," says the thin man, deadly serious.

"Oh come on, we have the best scientific brains in

the world here. They know exactly what they're doing," scoffs the disembodied voice.

The woman called Gabriela laughs bitterly.

"Oh right, like the Manhattan Project? Robert Oppenheimer was given the go ahead to start detonating hydrogen bombs on the Japanese before they knew whether or not the chain reaction would turn the earth into the sun in one giant nuclear chain reaction. They most definitely did not have all the answers."

Receiving no objection or comment from the interrogator, the man called Rafael continues.

"And the Hadron Collider. They have no idea what they could create. If they accidentally get it right in that facility in Switzerland they will recreate the moment the universe came into existence. Something which is still blowing apart who knows how many billions of years later? They might make time stand still or space fold in on itself."

Rafael tosses the hair out of his eyes in disgust.

Colonel Hassan sighs.

"There's nothing more dangerous, or pathetic, than a little knowledge."

Gabriela interrupts her antagonist.

"Is that right? This place is more dangerous than Oppenheimer's nuclear bomb and the Collider combined. Look what you've done to the weather around the world in your efforts to control it and extend growing seasons and mess up your enemies with earthquakes and tidal waves. Whole continents affected. And the whales and dolphins being washed up dead from the military blasting all those low frequency radio waves through the oceans so your nuclear subs need never surface to talk to you and give away their positions. Tut, tut."

Rafael continues.

"You are going to create a tear in time itself and then really weird shit will happen."

"As much as I would love to sit and listen to your bullshit all day, comic as it is, I really have to get some lunch," yawns Colonel Hassan.

"The beast is here you know?" asks Gabriela.

"Excuse me?"

"The beast of the pit. Abaddon. Our enemy of old. He's here," she replies.

The statement makes cold shivers run and up and down Gareth's back. And he realises there is another source of sound. He kills the video so he can hear it more clearly. It's the harp again. He doesn't move. The music from the harp seems to be coming from a long way off. Gareth wheels round and moves into the hall.

It sounds closer. It seems to be coming from the elevator shaft. Gareth tentatively edges closer to the entrance to the elevator under the sweeping staircase, but as he creeps nearer the sound suddenly stops.

He switches on his headlights and the bright beams pick out the five slack climbing ropes hanging from the steel pole which makes up the freight elevator's structure.

Gareth's wheelchair remains motionless as he looks at the ropes. One of them has started to swing slightly. Someone is climbing up. The rope pulls taught and starts to creak slightly as it is stretched. The walkie talkie on Gareth's lap makes a garbled electronic squeak and then falls silent once again.

# Michael

Gareth transmits, "Dad, Ted? Is that you climbing up the rope?"

Nothing.

"Can you hear me?"

Gareth waits, listening. There is no response but the rope keeps swinging rhythmically as the weight of a body continues its ascent.

Gareth starts to roll back very slowly from the elevator shaft in anticipation of whoever, or whatever, appears through the inspection flap in the base of the elevator car and is something other than a familiar face. Light starts to flicker through the flap in the floor of the elevator in an irregular patter and dances across the base of the stairs and the walls.

Then two strange things happen. The rope stops swinging and goes slack. And the flickering light becomes an intensifying pool on the ceiling as if the source is now heading straight up in the elevator. Which isn't possible as the elevator car is stationary in front of Gareth's eyes.

Gareth continues to retreat and parks in the shadows at the opposite end of the hall where he won't be seen by whoever, or whatever, appears through the bottom of the elevator car. A few seconds later, a hand—a human one he is relieved to see—followed by a second appear through the flap, then a white blonde shock of thick hair.

It's the man from the video who said all the things about God and the devil. He has a pencil torch in his mouth which he takes out and wipes his lips with the back of one enormous hand.

The rest of his form reveals itself through the flap and Gareth notices how smooth his movement is and how surprisingly tall he is. It's as if he is being raised on some sort of hidden hydraulic ramp. Or he can fly. The blonde man pats himself down and straightens his black roll-neck pullover. He must be nearly seven feet tall, Gareth thinks to himself. He doesn't so much look around as do some sort of inhuman radar sweep of the hall. As if he was a robot or an alien.

It's the peculiar movement where his eyes don't move at the same rate as his head which unnerves Gareth. It makes him look like a reptile. Then the blonde man breathes in very slowly and exhales through his mouth in a long sigh. He rubs his hands together as if he is cold and blows on the cupped hands. He raises his hands and exhales again as if he is blowing someone a kiss.

He stands stock still, listening for something. Gareth fully expects to be spotted any second but the blonde man moves off abruptly and disappears into the kitchen. He makes no sound. No footsteps. Nothing.

He's in the kitchen now, thinks Gareth. With Eli. Has he come to save him or kill him? Gareth doesn't move his wheelchair. What should he do? If he uses the walkie talkie again he will hear him.

What's happened to the others anyway? Has he killed them and come to kill Eli and then me?

And if he confronts the blonde man what can he do if he does bear malicious intent? Am I going to stab him with the titanium probe? Run him over? I don't think so, Gareth thinks feeling helpless. But he seemed very friendly in the camera clip, didn't he? I'm just being chicken.

And he was the one being held prisoner, not the anonymous military guy who was asking the questions. And his answers were really strange weren't they? As if he had tapped into something other people don't know about. How did he escape from those chains? Maybe Ted and Trent found him and released him to get help? What should I do?

"Why don't you ask him darling?"

The woman's voice whispers in his left ear from an impossible space between him and the wooden panelling of the two hundred year-old wall of the castle. Gareth's eyes widen in surprise and fear. The sudden sound of the terrifying disembodied voice has a galvanising effect on Gareth and he whirrs forward out of the shadows.

The blonde man is leaning over a very sick-looking Eli who is continuing to lose blood. It drips off the wooden surface around his prostrate body. The blonde man is checking Eli's pulse and has his other hand on his forehead. He speaks without turning round to face Gareth, who is in the kitchen doorway.

"Hallo Gareth. They said you were up here. I'm Michael. We can get to know each other a little more once we have Eli here stable."

Michael, the blonde man, turns his head briefly to look right at Gareth who says nothing and remains where he is. He has the bluest eyes Gareth has ever seen.

"They said you were a chatterbox. Look, I'm going to get Eli into the elevator and down to the basement where there is a fully-equipped emergency room. I need to do that now or your friend Eli here is going to die. But you need to trust me. And I need to borrow your transport if you don't mind."

Gareth backs away instinctively in his wheelchair until only his feet and the front wheels protrude across the threshold into the darkened kitchen.

"Why? You could be anyone. Where's my dad?" intones Gareth flatly through the synthesiser which belies the tension and fear he is feeling. Only his eyes communicate the emotions coursing through the stone statue of his body.

"They are preparing the ER for Eli and I to return," replies Michael matter of factly.

"Are you going to kill me?" asks Gareth with an enforced neutrality so at odds with the enormity of the question.

Michael stops what he is doing and turns to face Gareth.

"I'm here to save him and you Gareth. And we don't have time for this. Please come here."

Gareth holds Michael's gaze and then makes a decision. He rolls into the kitchen and comes to a halt next to where Michael is standing next to the unconscious Eli.

"Excuse me," says Michael softly as he rotates the release star in the centre of Gareth's five point racing harness. The metal clasps on the nylon padded belts pop open and fall away. Michael scoops up Gareth who is only a few pounds heavier than when he first suffered the paralysis at 12 years old and swings him round carefully into a nearby high-backed leather chair.

"This will be your temporary home just for five minutes, no more. I know where the emergency batteries for the elevator are and it will take no time at all for someone to be back for you. Thank you Gareth, you are going to save Eli's life."

The freakishly-tall man picks up Eli effortlessly and lowers him into Gareth's wheelchair, which is a tight fit. Eli's feet reach to the floor so Michael reverses out of the kitchen by pulling the wheelchair backwards and allowing Eli's feet to drag slightly. Eli's arms hang down lifelessly and his head flops against the head restraints which keep Gareth's head from doing the same.

"Don't get blood on it," says Gareth drily to Michael's back.

Completely helpless, Gareth watches them disappear. He has never felt more alone or vulnerable. How exactly did he get into this mess? he asks himself. The metronomic metallic tick of the clock in the hall echoes through the castle and into the kitchen. Gareth hears the low hum of the elevator. Well at least he was telling the truth about that part but more than that Gareth is at a loss to fathom. The way he seemed to float up out of the elevator shaft, the weird manner he looked around and the blowing. Why would he do that?

The ticking of the clock is quite annoying, he decides. I wish it would just stop. And then, to his astonishment and horror, it does. There is silence apart from the wind moaning from outside.

For some reason, the spectral image floats into his mind of a sailor's wife standing on the cliffs at night. She is looking out to sea while she desperately hopes beyond hope that she will see the navigation lights of her husband's fishing trawler hove into view amongst the heaving waves of the storm-ravaged sea.

He can almost feel the salty spray of the sea as it climbs the chalky fingers of the cliffs. Where has the ticking of the clock gone? Then it is there again. Tick tock through the wind and crashing of the waves. The fisherman's wife wipes salty tears away from her freezing cheeks and turns to face Gareth who, much to his surprise, is now standing next to her on the cliff top. Standing. Not in his wheelchair.

Gareth looks down at the pale grey and dirty white of the chalk cliffs below them. The waves explode over the rocks. Gareth notices they are in the shape of a ghostly skull. Its mouth is open in a permanent silent scream.

The waves break over the rocks and the image of the skull has gone when they retreat. The crying woman slips her hand into Gareth's and squeezes it. He looks up at her and realises he is a child again.

"Will you do it with me darling?"

It is his mother's voice talking to him. He is standing at the top of the stairs holding a shotgun and his mother is clinging to the banister below him looking beseechingly into his eyes. Her hands are like claws.

"Let's go together," she says before toppling back and seeming to float away into space.

The moment lasts for what seems like an eternity before she thumps down onto the wooden floor at the bottom of the stairs and rolls onto her front, broken like a discarded doll. Her back is a red mass of blood.

Gareth's eyes open with a start. He must have fallen asleep for a few seconds, or maybe it was hours? He has no idea. He listens. The clock is not ticking its rhythmic pattern. There is silence apart from the muted sound of the wind.

Then in the middle of the silence there is the chilling sound of the harp playing its mournful simple sequence. The same sound as he heard before. The same sound which they heard coming deep from within the castle before they set foot in it.

Gareth is powerless. His breathing quickens and grows ragged. To his alarm, he feels his body start to tip forward out of the chair. Almost imperceptibly at first then faster. He keels forward helplessly and crashes to the floor where he lies with his face half-pressed against the cold surface of the lino. Grit and dirt works its way into his mouth and a sliver of drool mixes with it.

From some distance away, maybe in the great hall, Gareth hears a growl. His eyes widen in fear. There it is again, only closer. It sounds like it is in the hall just outside the entrance to the kitchen. Gareth tries unsuccessfully to control his breathing. He forces himself to hold the breath in so he can hear better. The growling, low, menacing and guttural, seems to be drawing closer in the darkness.

The wind-up camping lights cast a yellow pool of light around the breakfast island. A thin, sticky rivulet of Eli's blood has run across the lino and now mixes with the drool from Gareth's crushed mouth as he lies helpless and inert on the cold lino.

What if it's attracted by the smell of blood? It will lead it straight to him. He feels so exposed and for the second time in twenty-four hours, Gareth believes he is about to die. Ripped apart by the same beast which attacked Eli. How ironic that it will be the same blood it tasted once already which will lead it to me, thinks Gareth.

The growling starts again suddenly what feels like inches from his ear. This is it, Gareth thinks. Any second, razor sharp claws will slash into his flesh. Robin found snake skin scales in Eli's wounds. What if it is a huge lizard? There is an explosive panting now as well as the demonic, savage growling. Please...please...just do it. Make it quick. I can't cope with watching my own body being ripped apart.

There is a thud from behind Gareth. And then another.

"Shit, how does he get this through doorways?"

Ted's voice.

"Dude, what are you doing down there?"

Gareth feels rather than sees Ted's hands on his shoulders, then his arms. He is lifted up and rotated around. His wheelchair is in front of him and Ted lowers him into it. As soon as he reattaches the voice synthesiser, Gareth tumbles out a staccato flood of disconnected words.

"Left alone...monster...Michael...Ted...leave here now. Danger...kill us all...Greg...my mother..."

Because the words are monotone, the intense fright Gareth has just experienced cannot convey the emotion as he grasps for the words.

"Whoa, slow down Cochise. What happened?" asks Ted kindly as he buckles Gareth back into his wheelchair and adjusts the eye sensor.

"Do you know who Michael is?" Gareth asks, ignoring Ted's question.

"Sure. He led us to the ER and we've been down there getting it ready for Eli. Michael's in there now with the others trying to save his life."

"But do you know who he actually is?" Gareth repeats the question.

"No, apart from he seems to know his way around down there and might save Eli's life."

"Don't you recognise him from the video?"

"Sure, and if he is a terrorist he's a really helpful one who seems to really love ex-soldiers."

# Eli

Under the yellow glare of emergency lights, the atmosphere in the ER is tense. No one speaks. Eli is connected to a saline drip and a dark red plasma bag. A heart monitor bleeps next to the cot.

Trent, Robin and Rachel are gathered round the foot of the cot while Michael injects something into Eli's arm. Michael works on the stab wound by cleaning it then carefully stitching the wound. He finishes by cleaning and dressing the area with fresh bandages.

Gareth and Ted are in the opposite corner. Ted is checking Gareth over thoroughly by gently running his hands down his arms and legs. He stares intently into Gareth's eyes from a few inches away, looking for a reaction.

"If there's anything broken I'll tell you. You don't have to stare at me like a freak," Gareth says finally.

"Just checking, dude." Ted ignores Gareth's sarcasm.

Satisfied, Ted straightens up and finds Trent and Rachel standing behind him.

"Are you OK, Gareth?" asks Rachel.

She looks strained and worried.

"I'm fine Rachel. How's Eli?" replies Gareth.

"He's doing better now we are getting some bloods and fluid into him but it's touch and go if he'll make it," says Trent quietly.

Rachel looks at her husband and she touches his arm tenderly. Trent hangs his head and looks ready to give in for the first time. Gareth has never seen him look so defeated.

"Come on dad, chin up. Eli's tough. He'll make it."

Gareth's attempt at reviving his father's spirits has no visible effect. Trent runs his hands through his hair and turns to walk over to Eli again. He bends down and puts a hand on Eli's shoulder.

He glances up at Michael who stands six inches taller than even Trent, the tallest amongst them.

"Will he make it?"

"That is in the lap of the gods."

Michael peels off the surgical gloves he is wearing and tosses them in the bin.

"He is going to need more blood than is stored here and there's no guarantee what we've got isn't going to kill him anyway with the constant loss of power and therefore refrigeration."

Gareth is behind Michael and his father. Gareth is staring at Michael and, sensing Gareth's eyes boring into his back, Michael turns round to face Gareth. Wordlessly, Michael settles back against the foot of the cot and folds his arms.

Gareth starts to speak, "Michael who...", and stops. A sharp whistling sound starts to ring in Gareth's ears and he finds he can't speak anymore.

The others don't appear to be able to hear the terrible noise which is like a high-pitched dentist's drill suddenly shrieking in Gareth's head.

Rula steps forward between Michael and Gareth and asks, "Gareth? Are you alright. What's the matter?"

Michael, looking concerned, straightens up and leans forward. As soon as he touches Gareth's arm, the awful screaming in Gareth's head stops.

"I'm...fine," responds Gareth.

"Was there something you wanted to ask?"

Michael slowly lowers himself into a chair next to Gareth's wheelchair. He is so tall he makes the chair appear more suitable for a child.

"I-I want to know who you are. Why did they take you prisoner and what are you doing here? And what is this place?"

Michael takes a deep breath and sighs.

"It's a long story Gareth."

"I'm a good listener," Gareth states flatly.

Michael puts a hand on either arm of the wheelchair and pulls it forward so they are facing each other. He gets close enough to prevent the others from hearing. They are all so focussed on Eli's condition they are not paying attention anyway.

Michael explains he was being held against his will for several weeks. No daylight, so the total length of time may have been longer, he's not sure. What the military were doing was illegal as he was being held against his wishes. He and the others, Gabriela, Rafael and Uri—the man who Gareth saw being choked to death by the invisible force—did get onto the research base by illegally breaking through the perimeter fence so they were committing an offence. They knew the risk they were running.

They also knew the danger the experiment being run on the base—and dozens like it around the world—posed to the planet.

"That's a bold statement Michael," observes Gareth. "What is the experiment you are all so scared of and who exactly are you? You still haven't really told any of us."

Michael compresses his lips in thought and studies Gareth's expressionless face.

"So much emotion and such a fine intellect," he says, almost regretfully.

"You seem sad. Isn't it a good thing to be brainy and have feelings?" retorts Gareth.

"You and I are alike Gareth. We are both trapped but for very different reasons," Michael replies sadly.

"What do you mean?" asks Gareth.

Michael doesn't answer his question. Instead he continues his explanation by describing the organisation the activists including him are part of. They have infiltrated three of the eighteen sites around the world simultaneously to embarrass the authorities and bring the experiment into the headlines from the shadows.

"You still haven't told me what the experiment is," prompts Gareth.

"You have to be prepared to put aside whatever perceptions you may have about how much the authorities tell you and what their priorities are," Michael says conspiratorially.

"I'm listening," Gareth says.

Michael describes a global experiment to alter the weather to combat climate change.

"It is sponsored by a world order who also control the world's banks, the energy companies and even the Federal Reserve. They are using a system called HAARP. It stands for High Frequency Active Auroral Programme. It was originally developed to help find oil reserves by transmitting low frequency radio waves into the ground which showed up reserves of oil and gas. It didn't require planting explosives to seismically show where the oil was and could even be used from the air—useful in the Arctic or over oceans.

"It is based on theories that Nikola Tesla, a brilliant Serbian inventor from the early twentieth century, wrote about. He believed that a targeted powerful beam of energy could be used to penetrate water to communicate with submarines without them having to surface, as radio waves traditionally couldn't penetrate water. He thought that the same type of extremely low frequency radio waves could be used to heat the atmosphere and therefore change the earth's weather, and even trigger earthquakes by resonating at exactly the same frequency as the earth, two point five gigahertz."

"Amazingly," Michael continues, "research carried out recently by scientists has proved his theories correct. Even down to heating the upper atmosphere to make it bulge higher up into lower space where a whole generation of communication satellites are in low orbit above the earth. The drag from increasing the higher levels of even such a thin sliver of atmosphere is enough to degrade their orbit and make them crash at will. So if one country thinks another is spying on them too much, they can bring the satellite down without any evidence. They even use it for assessing the composition of the moon and remember about looking for oil? They're using it for looking for Iran's underground network of tunnels now. That's where they're building their nuclear weapons. Scientists have started to utilise it to experiment with geo-engineering."

"What's that?" interrupts Gareth. Throughout this exchange, Michael has held Gareth in his gaze almost as if he is hypnotised.

"It's weather engineering. It started with cloud seeding to make it rain where there was drought. Now they are trying to slow down the speed the earth's weather is changing but it is still a very inexact science.

The scientists are so focussed on the task in hand to increase rainfall, extend the growing season and maximise crop yields, they don't connect it with the millions of fish which are killed each time they target the ocean. They don't understand it is also the cause for migrating whales and dolphins beaching themselves or the birds which suddenly drop out of the air in their thousands. They don't realise they have tapped into the force which created everything. They have released God's power. That wasn't the plan."

"What plan?" asks Gareth.

"God's plan for man. He was supposed to use it for space and time travel like nuclear power but instead as with nuclear power he has become obsessed with using it for dominating his fellow man. Such a disappointment."

"How do you know? Are you and God best buddies or something?" asks Gareth, thinking back to Michael's levitation trick in the elevator.

"Not exactly but I've...done my research," smiles Michael. "This power is God's power. The power that is held in the Ark of the Covenant. The Ark of the Covenant generated this power. Now the Ark is in the hands of the beast."

"Who?" prompts Gareth.

"Abaddon. The beast of the pit. He has the Ark and he shared the secret of how to create the power to the Nephilim here on earth in this dimension."

Michael's eyes are looking right through Gareth and he seems unaware he is talking to him.

"You're so losing me," interjects Gareth.

Michael's eyes refocus on Gareth.

"My apologies. While running a test over Indonesia in two thousand and four, they triggered an earthquake on a fault line eight hundred and fifty miles along down the west coast of the Indonesian islands. Eight hundred and fifty miles of seabed rose up forty metres in twenty seconds and triggered the largest tsunami on record."

"Did they stop when they realised what they'd done?" Gareth asks emotionlessly.

"No that was, is, the problem. Worse, it started affecting other sensitive areas because of something called dynamic triggering. One earthquake would literally trigger the next. Which is why we've had so many big ones in such a short time. Even the volcano in Iceland. The fault lines are all connected. It became part of the experiment because they realised they had stumbled on the perfect weapon which, very conveniently, also came with total deniability.

"The political situation in Asia has become a security issue for the west. Until now North Korea, unlike Iraq, Afghanistan and Cuba, have ignored these people's demands to accept their banking and governance. Japan and China are enemies historically and the rest of the region has been overrun by the communists, the traditional enemies of the west. When the west discovered Japan was producing enriched uranium and turning it into plutonium, which is what they use to make nuclear weapons, and were selling it to Iran, something deniable but effective had to be done to stop it.

"Japan sits on one of the biggest fault lines in the world and so they triggered an earthquake. They heated the ionosphere above the Sea of Japan and created a massive area of low pressure—like you get before a hurricane. Trillions of tons of water expanded upwards—handy for flooding sea defences—and that had the effect of putting less pressure on the sea bed. Two opposing bands of rock pushing against one another on that same seabed with almost unimaginable force can suddenly move and release the entire load which has built up."

"What happened?" asks Gareth, struggling to keep up with such a dense download of complex information.

"Bam! Earthquake!" Michael claps his hands together. Gareth doesn't react. He continues staring at Michael.

Startled, the others turn round from where they are leaning over Eli.

"What's going on?" asks Trent, annoyed.

Gareth rotates his chair away from Michael's hold to face his father.

"Michael has just been explaining how much shit we're in. Do you know anyone at the US Defense Department?" Gareth says flatly.

"I know the guy who wrote the exit strategy for the US for Iraq," replies Trent. "Trouble is, he's a Colonel in the British Army but he might know someone. Why?"

"We're sitting on God's bomb right here, according to Michael," replies Gareth.

Michael stands up to his full imposing height and folds his muscular arms in an easy pose behind Gareth's wheelchair.

Rula has been watching the exchange and she indicates Michael with a toss of her head.

"Why should we trust what this guy says? He looks like a reptile and he sounds like a snake."

"Or a lizard," agrees Robin.

Rachel is sitting on Eli's bed, studying Eli's injuries. She doesn't even look up.

"I apologise for my very rude friends Michael but

that's the first time they have agreed on anything which is worth celebrating. Hopefully we'll have time for that later. Before that we have more serious matters to attend to. Robin can you come and look at Eli? The infection seems to be getting worse."

Robin checks over Eli's multiple cuts which have formed bloody, ragged crusts. Some are now weeping an evil-looking yellow pus.

"They are becoming infected," she nods.

Trent turns to Michael.

"Is it possible there are any more medical supplies stored somewhere else?"

Michael shrugs.

"Possible but unlikely. When I escaped I had a thorough look around and can't remember seeing any antibiotics then. But then it is dark down here."

Robin is studying Michael's face for any tell-tale signs of lying but finds none.

"How did you escape again? And what happened?" she asks.

Michael doesn't appear to hear her.

"Can I suggest maybe Ted and Robin come and look with me? I think there may be-"

Trent interrupts.

"I have a better idea. Ted, why don't you come with Rula and me? We'll see if we can make the elevator work more reliably so we can deliver Eli to people who will make him better."

Gareth rolls over to his father and blocks his way in his version of a protest.

"Someone is staying here with me this time. No arguments."

Trent looks at his son as if for the first time and registers something new about him. Trent nods and looks to Rachel quizzically.

"Sure. I'll stay here with Gareth and keep an eye on Eli. Don't be too long."

Rachel settles herself into the chair by Eli's cot.

"Ted? Please can you and Rula come with me then as I suggested? We should get topside in case anyone has found us. They'd never know we were down here," asks Trent.

Then he strides out of the ER without even checking to see if the others are following him. Ted and Rula look at each other, and then silently follow Trent out of the room.

They follow him down the darkened corridor to the elevator. The only illumination is from the head torches they all wear. The trio of beams bob around as they walk. They reach the elevator and Ted slides up the safety cage. He and Rula step in. Trent hangs back and gesticulates for them to go.

"I'll stay here and keep guard to make sure nothing follows you up there."

Ted looks at Trent, surprised at this development. He assumed they would all go together.

"Are you sure?" Ted asks him searchingly.

"I thought the idea was to stay together? It doesn't feel right to me."

Trent shrugs and waves them off.

"Go on you two. I thought you might appreciate some time alone."

"Oh so that's it," Rula smiles. "You're not quite the lump of wood I've always taken you for, Trent."

"Thanks, you ungrateful cow."

Trent smiles as he slides the safety cage down and presses the button to send them upwards.

At exactly the same time as ted and Rula step into the elevator, Gareth is looking into Eli's face as he sleeps. The injured ex-Navy Seal is breathing shallowly but rhythmically and seems more stable to Gareth's amateur eye. Rachel has fallen instantly into the sort of deep sleep only complete exhaustion brings in the chair next to Eli's cot.

Gareth reflects on the bizarre chain of events which have taken place over the last forty-eight hours and how all their lives will never be the same as long as they live.

Eli's eyes open suddenly and focus on Gareth.

"Hello Greg."

It's his mother.

Eli's lips are moving but it is his mother speaking. The ER emergency lighting casts a yellow glare across the handsome features of the ex-soldier. Pus from Eli's wounds begins to ooze more freely, soaking his clothes once again. Small pieces of the crusts on the wounds break free and join the disgusting flow onto the floor.

Gareth's eyes are wide with fear and he looks at Rachel to see if the voice has woken her but she continues sleeping peacefully. He is too terrified to speak or move his wheelchair and he fixes his gaze on the strange rictus which has taken charge of Eli's features. His face is frozen into a sort of death mask grin and he is staring directly at Gareth despite the yellowy gloom in the room.

"This is the last time I can speak to you Greg."

Gareth finally finds his voice again.

"Why don't you leave me alone? What are you doing in Eli's body?"

"Eli isn't here anymore. We're the only reason he's still breathing. When we go, he dies."

"No!"

Delissa's soft voice suddenly becomes a horrible guttural snarl.

"It doesn't matter what happens to this cuntish filth."

Then Delissa is there again, but her voice goes from soft to whiny and threatening.

"It's of no importance. I have something I must tell you. I wanted to tell you before. Your father knows, so does that bitch whore he married. You should be dead Greg, like me. But you're not. Do you remember why? Or have you forgotten everything?"

"I don't trust you. Who are you really?" asks Gareth in his flat tone.

"We are everything you filthy fucking boy whore. You lay with your own mother! Don't you remember?"

The guttural male snarl is back. It laughs with an insane cackling glee and Eli's body starts thrusting lasciviously, its hips splatting wetly back onto the cot in a spreading pool of blood and pus. Some of it splashes across Gareth's face. He is powerless to do anything about it as it drips slowly down his white, sweating face.

"Please leave us alone. Why are you hurting us?" asks Gareth.

It's Delissa again, composed and gentle.

"I want revenge for what you did. For what your father did."

"What have we done?" asks Gareth insistently.

Eli/Delissa looks at him expectantly, as if she is waiting for him to remember.

"Don't remember? No? Let me jog your memory."

Eli stands up, pulling over the drips inserted into his arms as he does so. He yanks the tubes out of his arms and turns his back to Gareth.

"See?"

Eli's back is a red mass of blood and the rear of his head is shot away. He settles back on the bed. Gareth is reversing, very slowly, toward the open door.

"You shot me with your daddy's gun, Greg. You shot me and I died. I wasn't ready to die and now I'm stuck here in hell. Waiting for you."

Then Eli's chest caves in as if an invisible weight has started pressing on it. He starts to choke and fight for breath. His hands fly up to his throat and he claws at it. He looks imploringly at Gareth.

"Help me Gareth. Do something," Eli gasps in his own voice through his clenched fists. Gareth can see it's Eli in his eyes. The spirits have gone or retreated.

Gareth's eyes flick alternately between Rachel, who is motionless and still sleeping deeply, and Eli, who is choking to death in front of him. Gareth rolls his wheelchair forward and bumps impotently into the bed and then he retreats. He crashes his wheelchair much harder into the bed again then reverses, turns round, and runs directly into Rachel. She doesn't react. It's as if she is dead.

# Gates

Ted raises his hand and brushes away a non-existent strand of Rula's hair from her face. As the elevator whirrs upwards through the darkness they move closer to each other and Rula slips her arms round Ted's waist.

"How thoughtful of Trent to give us this moment together," she breathes into his ear.

"Very thoughtful," nods Ted as he kisses her up-turned mouth through his soft, bushy beard. Rula cups his big face in her hands and kisses him back, more urgently this time.

They kiss passionately as Ted puts his strong, gentle hands on her back and pulls her closer to him. They have reached the ground floor of the castle and, as the car comes to a halt, the cage door shoots up without Ted having to do it.

There are four armed soldiers standing facing them and they freeze in mid-embrace.

Before they can speak, the two soldiers standing nearest them open fire and they are blasted back against the far side of the elevator cage. Ted and Rula slump lifelessly to the floor.

"Get them out of there," snaps a voice dismissively from behind the four soldiers. A voice which is clearly used to being obeyed.

It belongs to another soldier who is clearly an officer. He has two gold stars on his epaulettes, indicating the status of a US army general.

Ted and Rula, two flesh and blood people with homes, families, a past and a future up until a few seconds ago, are dragged from where they have fallen and discarded casually like kitchen scraps. The four soldiers and the general step forward into the elevator, drop the cage door and start to descend.

∪∪∪

Simultaneously, Trent, waiting at the bottom of the shaft, hears the shots and, horrified, cranes his neck up to try and catch a glimpse of the reason for the sudden gunfire. Seeing the winch cable descending and the hum of the motor, he turns and sprints away fast down the corridor.

He bursts in to the ER and is met with the sight of Eli spread-eagled in a grotesque tableau of death. The shock of finding his best friend dead is too much for Trent. He sobs and bites his hand as tears spring from his eyes and run freely down his face. Then he notices Rachel in the gloom who looks as if she in some sort of trance or coma. She has slumped sideways at an impossibly uncomfortable angle. No one could sleep like that.

There is no sign of Gareth.

Trent hears the sound of the cage crashing open at the other end of the corridor. He tries to wake Rachel by shaking her violently and calling her name but there is no response. He can hear the soldiers' boots on the linoleum approaching the ER. He knows it will be the first place they will look and he assumes they will execute anyone and everyone they find.

As the soldiers burst into the ER they take in the sight of Eli lying dead in a thickening pool of his own blood and greenish yellow pus which is running in viscous rivulets from the cot onto the lino floor. Rachel is slumped sideways, oblivious. They look around but there is no one else present.

"There are four of them including the boy in the wheelchair. Correction—three," states the officer, looking dispassionately at Eli.

General Gates is not a patient or sympathetic man. His detractors would argue a case for him having the personality traits of a sociopath. Not someone you would ever want to make angry.

His operation at the Defense Department is so secret only a handful of the military know of its existence. Complete deniability. This recent breach of security and the resulting sudden silence from their top secret facility has created a serious dilemma for him. He has staked his entire career, a very successful one in black ops with the CIA, on this operation to get the upper hand in weather weaponisation and disruption ahead of the Chinese and the Russians.

If the existence of this advanced facility utilising the technology of HAARP—the High Frequency Active Auroral Research Programme—to determine how a targeted radio beam 72,000 times more powerful than the biggest radio station beacon in the world can be weaponised is revealed, Gates and his small team will be vaporised and their existence airbrushed from the records.

His scientists, all educated at Massachusetts Institute of Technology, London's Imperial College and other stars in the cutting edge of technology, have made a breakthrough of such significance in the science that the world will want a piece of it and the brains behind it.

They have discovered the doomsday machine. The ultimate weapon.

A weapon which can silently disrupt a tectonic plate of your choosing and create a mega-earthquake, or change the path of the Jetstream and cause a five year winter or summer, or create floods and hurricanes in the region of your choice. All with total deniability.

The side-effects are still being assessed. One of which is a strange, localised power black-out at night for some reason they haven't conquered as yet and another was a slowing or reversal in actual time itself. This is being monitored at the castle facility by an atomic clock of the kind held at Greenwich Observatory in London which is used for setting Greenwich Mean Time and all the world's time zones.

Atomic clocks are accurate to a millionth of a second, so any change in the passage of time, or the rotation of the earth and therefore the length of an earth day, is detected in microscopic detail.

The latest experiment had been to see what happens when the magnetosphere, the protective electromagnetic field miles above the earth, is bombarded. A sudden upheaval in the weather has resulted. Not something anyone would want to be caught being responsible for. And now Gates has to deal with the reason for this sudden communication blackout from the castle research facility.

Heads were going to roll, Gates would see to that.

Struggling to slow his rapid breathing, Trent watches Gates and the four soldiers from where he has squeezed into the air conditioning duct above the ER into which he has dragged himself.

He disappeared just in time before Gates made his entrance.

His fists tighten into balls as he sees the general prod his wife in an attempt to wake her to no avail. Under instruction from the general, the soldiers pick up the inert body of what had been Eli, Trent's best friend. The man who shot his way through a gang of heavily-armed Taliban and saved Trent from capture and probable execution is dragged unceremoniously out of the ER by his feet, leaving a dark yellow and red streak on the floor as they do so. Rachel is manhandled by the second pair of soldiers who carry her out after Eli, followed by Gates.

Trent waits, motionless, until he is certain they have gone and he can no longer hear their voices or grunts of exertion. Almost silently, he lifts the dislodged vent and puts it to one side, then lowers himself back into the room.

He replaces the vent and goes to the door to listen. His mind is racing. He needs to find where they are taking Rachel and then reconnect with Michael, Robin and Gareth as at the moment he has no idea where any of them are.

Using his torch headlight will give his presence away to the soldiers immediately, so Trent creeps silently along the corridor away from the elevator in almost pitch black. The only light is from luminous discs which surround all the regular corridor lights set into the ceiling and walls.

They cast an eerie green glow across Trent's face and he can just about make out his own hands in the gloom. Trent slides slowly along the wall, feeling his way across the rough seams of the breeze blocks which make up the walls. He comes to the doorway of the video room where Gareth found the video camera on his first foray into the basement.

The hairs on the back of his neck start to prickle as he hears shallow breathing which is not his.

"Trent, is that you?"

An urgent hiss which he recognises as Michael's voice comes from the video room.

"Yes. Who's with you?" Trent fires back.

"Me. Thank fuck. We just saw some army guys carrying Rachel and Eli."

It's Robin.

Trent slips quickly into the video room. He can make out Michael's shock of white blonde hair but nothing else as it's so dark. More by feel than sight Trent finds his way to where the others are crouching beneath the vision mixing desk.

Robin grabs Trent by the arm and gasps, "Who are those guys? I think we heard shots. Are they going to kill us?"

Trent puts his arm around Robin and holds her until her ragged breathing slows.

"Robin, Michael. Ted and Rula are dead, shot. Eli died while we were over at the elevator. Rachel's in a coma and Gareth's disappeared."

Michael uncoils his near seven-foot frame a little and runs his hands through his thick blonde hair a few times as he reacts to the news.

"I think a lot of people have already died and this is just a continuation of that mopping-up procedure. We need to save ourselves if we can."

Robin throws her head back in disgust and whispers at Michael in a barely-contained fury, "Those were people I loved you heartless fucking bastard. Is that all the price of a life is worth to you?"

Michael doesn't react.

"I'm being practical. Thinking how to save your life

and ours. These men intend to kill us."

Trent nods.

"Michael's right Robin. We are in terrible danger and we need to think how to get out of here alive. There are five armed men walking around who just shot Ted and Rula in cold blood. They are not operating within the normal rules I can assure you. They don't want anyone to know about this place and they will kill to keep it that way."

Robin ejects herself from her hiding place and goes over to the door which she closes carefully.

"Our voices will carry much further than we think. Right, tell me what you think our exit strategy is then."

Gareth rolls forward in the wheelchair. His mind has unravelled almost totally since that demon or whatever it was started talking to him through Eli. He really can't think straight any longer. He has no idea where he is. He is trying without much success to process what it said.

He is really Greg, not Gareth, and he doesn't even exist apparently. He never had a twin who he made up. But he has memories of Greg. Like when they caught a butterfly in a net and put the butterfly in a bell-jar. It had the most beautiful colouring he had ever seen and Greg said the same...didn't he?

He struggles to remember the moment properly. Was there another person with him or was Greg actually him talking to himself in his own mind? Just like I am now!

He is called Gareth. He knows he is. He has always been called Gareth. That creature was taunting him, trying to confuse him for some evil purpose which

Gareth may never understand. But it knew Delissa's name and it spoke to him in the darkness. He didn't imagine that at least. Or did he?

Rachel was there when it happened, wasn't she? Oh wait, she was in a bloody coma and didn't hear or see anything. But it stood up and showed him Eli's back. And what about the dream when he saw his mother on the stairs? He had no recollection of that ever happening but now it was imprinted in his memory it felt like fact.

Gareth is so deeply distracted by the confusing thoughts coursing through his mind and the trauma of what he just witnessed that he has lost track of where he is. He hasn't noticed that he has entered the recreation centre for the facility, which has a 25 metre swimming pool as its centrepiece.

🏛️🏛️🏛️

Trent, Michael and Robin are flattened against a breezeblock wall.

Their silhouettes are framed by the luminous emergency coils in the ceiling. Bright pencil beams of light are dancing down the corridor to their right as the soldiers are approaching. Trent's hand falls on a door handle and he presses it down as quietly as he can. It creaks complainingly but the door gives and he pulls the others inside with him.

As they stumble backwards they fall over something on the floor and collapse on top of it. In the near-darkness Robin realises they have just fallen on a pile of bodies. She is about to scream when Michael's hand clamps over her mouth, stifling the sound.

He whispers into her ear without releasing the pressure of his hand over her mouth, "Welcome to Dante's

Inferno. Hell on earth."

They slither off the disgusting pile of bodies and prostrate themselves on the floor.

"They're coming this way," whispers Trent. "Get amongst the bodies and lie still," he orders.

Michael and Trent push their way under the untidy array of arms and legs. Robin hesitates for a second with a look of revulsion on her face. The voices of the soldiers and the beams from their flashlights are getting closer. Then the door handle starts moving.

Someone is entering the room.

Robin slides under the pile of bodies and lays still with the other two. A beam of light passes over them. She can hear breathing which is easy as she is holding her own. They sound close enough to touch her. Her eyes are shut as she plays dead as best she can. She is dependent on her hearing for vectoring where the soldiers are in the room. There is a blinding blur from a flashlight which dazzles her, even through her closed eyelids.

"Someone has done the job for us," observes one voice.

"These aren't the ones we're looking for. They're hiding from us. The kid in the wheelchair should be easy to find though," gloats the other.

Failing to notice the three additional bodies, the voices start to withdraw. As they are leaving the room the owner of the first voice says conversationally, "Gates says we are going to interrogate them before we get rid of them."

"Category Three Prisoners?" asks the second voice nonchalantly.

"Category Three. Any means necessary."

The door closes.

🪕🪕🪕

Gareth realises too late that he is actually moving along the edge of a swimming pool in his wheelchair. Just before one set of wheels drops over the ledge he swerves to the left away from the inky blackness.

But the movement is so violent that the wheelchair overbalances and tips on its side next to the pool. From the moment he was returned to his wheelchair everyone had failed to notice his harness had not been done up. Gareth is hurled out and lands like a sack of potatoes on the cold, hard surface of the tiles surrounding the pool. His momentum rolls him forward just enough to teeter on the edge of the tiles over the black water.

Gareth stares silently down at the perfect flat sheen of the water. For a second he thinks he is at least safe from falling into the water but his body weight is forward just enough to tip him in.

He disappears beneath the surface with a soft plop.

At first the cold water is a shock. Gareth can't see anything, just wet blackness. How long can he hold his breath before he drowns? he wonders calmly to himself. Why am I so calm? I'm going to die. It can't be that bad, certainly no worse than what life has become over the last few hours. They are all going to die anyway. Whatever diabolical force has been unleashed here is never going to let them leave. No one is ever going to get out alive. So this is not too bad, better even.

But he doesn't want to feel the rush of cold chlorinated water entering his lungs. He's frightened of the moment when he is going to release the air in his lungs and involuntarily gasp for breath except only water will rush into his mouth and down and into his lungs. He wonders how long it will take for him to lose consciousness after that. Will he be dead immediately or will there be a sort of handover period where he is neither dead or alive? Where it could go either way between life and death?

He realises he is starting to sink ever so slowly, as he can feel the water caressing his face and hands. He starts to accelerate almost imperceptibly. Because he can't see a thing, he's unable to tell if he is on his back, or even if he is pointing down like the free diver video he saw on YouTube once.

The man simply stepped off a ledge in chest deep water and dropped headfirst into a natural underwater cavern. He sailed gracefully downwards for one hundred metres. When he reached the sandy bottom, he simply hauled himself back to the surface by gliding weightlessly up the wall of the cavern like Spiderman.

If only I could do that, Gareth thinks. Then something nudges him out of his reverie. Unseen hands below him are holding him very gently and he can feel from the direction of the water that he is starting to rise upwards like the free diver in the video.

At least he thinks it's upwards, as he has become completely disoriented in the darkness. It could just as easily be down. The power must have just come back on though. He can see a light shimmering and dancing through the water and he is moving towards it. His chest no longer feels as if it wants to burst from holding his breath. In fact the whole breathing issue has gone away altogether. Gareth realises he can't feel the water on his skin anymore.

The light has become clearer. It is a person. Or rather it's a person with wings. The beautiful shape flexes and Gareth can make out the huge feathers.

He realises he must still be in the water as a female form is floating towards him. He can make out her long black hair moving round her head like a small shoal of tiny fish. Her lifeless body rotates slowly like a space station in orbit around the earth. There is a sort of graceful beauty to her slow roll.

As she revolves to face him he recognises her features which are pale and blurred in the water. It's his mother Delissa. Her face is set in a gentle smile and her sightless eyes stare lifelessly at him. She turns away from him and Gareth is exposed to the hole blown out of the back of her head and the dark black blood seeping from between her shoulders.

Delissa drops away, or rather he moves past her. Gareth doesn't feel the cold terror which has gripped him in their previous ghostly encounters. It's as if...he searches in his mind for what it's like because it's unlike any emotion he has ever encountered. It's like he's watching someone else's life...as if it's a movie he could walk out of any time he wanted to. He doesn't feel in danger or threatened.

In fact he doesn't feel anything at all. The unseen hands continue to propel him gently upwards towards the light. There is the body of a young boy floating spread-eagled above him. His hair is blonde, like Gareth's. As he drifts nearer, Gareth realises the boy is his double, only maybe twelve years or so younger.

My twin Greg? he wonders. But Delissa's ghost had told him he didn't have a twin and that his real name was Greg. But here's a boy who looks like him, but isn't him because his name is Gareth and he isn't dead yet, or at least he doesn't think he is. The blonde boy rolls gently in the water and Gareth feels he is looking at him. He rolls around and Gareth can see a large bloody hole in his back.

It takes Gareth several seconds to process what he

is looking at and then he recoils and starts to struggle. He can move his limbs. The boy is his twin Greg. And I shot him. At the same time as I shot my own mom.

Gareth tries to scream "No!" His mouth moves but the scream is still-born except for a noisy stream of bubbles. There is a figure in the light leaning down now. Hands enter the water trying frantically to grab hold of him. He inhales the water and his chest heaves spasmodically.

Gareth stops moving and starts to float downwards, away from the light and away from the reaching hands.

A figure dives into the water and swims down to Gareth and grabs him. The figure is joined by another with a glowing halo of blonde hair waving in the water. They haul Gareth's lifeless body to the surface. There is no light, just the same eerie darkness as before.

As Trent and Michael break the surface they both gasp for air. Trent has his arm supporting Michael's throat and chin. He keeps his airways clear of the dark, chilly water while they swim awkwardly to the side of the pool. Michael gets to the side first and ejects himself out of the water. He extends an arm to help pull Trent out and then, using their combined strength, they haul Gareth's limp body out as well.

Trent rolls Gareth on to his back. He tears his own t-shirt over his head and shoulders then rolls it into a makeshift pillow under Gareth's inert head. He bends down and presses his ear against Gareth's puny little chest and listens.

"I can't hear anything," Trent pants.

Michael has his thumb and forefinger on Gareth's wrist.

"No pulse."

Michael shakes his head.

"The boy mustn't die," says Michael, more to himself than Trent.

Trent glances at Michael, bewildered. Then he pinches Gareth's nose and exhales strongly but gently into Gareth's open mouth. He repeats the procedure twice more then listens again for signs of life.

"Still nothing. Shit."

"Let me try," urges Michael.

"No way. He's my son. I can save him."

Michael kneels down next to Trent and puts his arm across Trent, effectively blocking him.

"What the fuck are you doing?" Trent explodes and pushes Michael's arm away.

"Trent, do you want your son back?" asks Michael calmly.

"More than anything you stupid shit. Get out of my way," barks Trent and he pushes Michael again.

Michael says nothing. He rubs his hands together like he is trying get some warmth into them. Then he blows out a long, controlled breath and opens the palms of his hands onto Gareth's head.

Trent pushes his ear up against Gareth's chest instinctively and his screwed up eyes open wide.

"I can hear his heart," he shouts with astonishment.

Gareth heaves and a lot of water gushes out of his mouth. Then he coughs and starts to draw in big breaths of air. Trent puts his son in the recovery position and rubs his back while more water trickles from Gareth's mouth.

He looks at his father with confused eyes. A few seconds ago he was swimming for his life towards the light. He had been moving. It was glorious. Did he dream it? Was it another of his waking fantasies? Or did he nearly just die?

Gareth had read about near death experiences. People in car crashes or on the operating table had described walking towards an angel by a bridge of light and had been tempted to go with them. But for some reason they had changed their minds and chosen to go back. Then they had woken up thinking they had almost gone to heaven then returned.

Once Gareth's breathing has stabilised, Trent and Michael lift him and replace him in the relative safety and familiarity of his wheelchair. Reconnected to the voice synthesiser, Gareth can communicate with them.

"How long was I in the water?" Gareth asks through the monotone voice synthesiser.

"We walked into the pool room just as you slipped forward into the water," replies Trent.

"We had you out within about fifteen seconds," adds Michael.

They are all still dripping wet.

"I had some weird dreams," says Gareth flatly.

"You have always been one for weird dreams, son." Trent uses his discarded pullover to act as a rudimentary towel on Gareth. "We'll have you dry in no time."

"That won't be necessary," states a voice behind them.

They whirl round to be confronted with four raised semi-automatic guns levelled at them by the soldiers.

General Gates is pointing a pistol at Gareth.

"For terrorists you give away your position far, far too easily," he sneers.

Blinding flashlights flick on and dazzle them. Trent and Michael instinctively raise their arms to shield their eyes. Gareth screws his tight shut.

"You are now our...guests. Do not try to resist. Cuff them to the kid's wheelchair," barks Gates.

Two of the grunts shoulder their rifles and handcuff Trent and Michael to Gareth's wheelchair.

"You won't be able to go anywhere in a hurry now," smirks Gates, holstering his weapon.

# Robin

Robin watches the group of men as they pass below the aircon vent. She is small enough to wriggle through the eighteen-inch piping from room to room. She is the only one of the climbing party still free. That argument with Rula about the Palestinian question seems so long ago. Never in her most extreme moments would she have imagined hiding in an air vent from the very men who were supposed to defend people against murderous regimes precisely like the one they appeared to be working for.

Trent and Michael have one arm handcuffed to the rail on the back of Gareth's wheelchair. All three of them are wet but otherwise look unharmed. Robin instinctively dislikes Gates intensely. His hooded eyes and dark complexion make him resemble a bird of prey.

Robin was given her English name at boarding school because she was always tiny, fierce and hyperactive like the bird of the same name. She was named Reema—White Antelope—at home in Palestine but it became Robin when her parents moved to England.

The man who murdered her best friends will be punished for his wrongdoing, even if it means things turn out badly for her. But how? She is on her own and she has no weapon or means of attack. But hasn't she been in this position before when she was with the freedom fighters?

Desperation is the mother of invention.

She wriggles along the ducting on her elbows and knees. It's a tight squeeze and there would be no way a male would be able to do what she's doing. After what feels like hundreds of metres of crawling, Robin realises she is above one of the secure rooms.

By pressing her nose against the cold, hard slats of the ventilation grate she has a partial view of the room. Visibility is poor due to the ongoing power cut and the only illumination is from emergency lighting, which is minimal.

Once her eyes have adjusted, Robin can make out the supine form of Rachel who seems to be asleep. Robin hasn't seen Rachel since she left with Michael to look for supplies, leaving her with Eli and Gareth.

That was before Ted and Rula were executed in the elevator. It all seems like a very long time ago even though in reality it wasn't much more than an hour. Where are the others? she wonders to herself. Are they still alive or have they been executed? Robin can't see anyone else in the room.

She is toying with the idea of removing the grate and lowering herself into the room when her thought train is interrupted by the lock turning and the heavy door swinging open below.

Gates enters the room and stands over Rachel. After a few seconds, he nudges her with his foot but she doesn't wake up. He hesitates, weighing something up in his mind.

And then he bends down and runs his hands over Rachel's flat, toned stomach through her crumpled blouse. He stops, his hands still in place in the yellowy gloom. Robin's fists tighten involuntarily and she has to jam one of them into her mouth to stop herself from shouting out.

"Come on Rach, wake up," she mutters under breath.

Being the cool-headed thinker she is, Robin realises she may be the only one left not under lock and key and therefore the only hope any of them have of escape. After the way her friends were summarily executed, they clearly have a shoot to kill policy in place for any escapees—would be or otherwise. Someone very clearly does not want the secrets of the castle to be released to the outside world.

Gates, emboldened by the lack of reaction, moves his hands higher and he cups Rachel's breasts through her shirt. Slowly he starts to unbutton her blouse to reveal her naked breasts. He slides his meaty hands across them and rubs her nipples then one hand insinuates itself into the front of her pants and he starts to manipulate her between her legs in a disgusting display of sexual assault he believes to be unseen.

"You are going to suffer so much for this you dirty bastard," hisses Robin under her breath.

Gates withdraws his hands and starts to unzip his fly as he straddles Rachel with one leg. Robin, in desperation, reaches into her pocket and throws a small handful of loose change as far down the ventilation duct as he can. The coins land a room's length away and clatter metallically.

Gates leaps up in guilty surprise and starts yelling orders as he hastily zips his fly. Rachel is still immobile as if she is in some sort of coma. Robin carefully withdraws in the opposite direction to where the coins landed.

There is a series of deafening explosions and the screech of tearing metal as dozens of bullets rip through the ventilation duct and ricochet around her head.

The need for stealth now gone, Robin wriggles on all fours as fast as she is able backwards from the lethal scar of bullets tearing through the metal of the duct ten metres away. The shooting suddenly stops. She can hear Gates still barking orders at the four soldiers with the automatic weapons. She freezes.

They are listening to see if they can assess her position.

Slowly and carefully, she starts to move along the duct at a right angle to the route she has just come. Like a giant caterpillar, Robin hauls herself along away from her original position. She hears a noise which makes her blood chill. A loud metallic shrick tells her someone has pushed one of the ventilation grates in.

She can hear someone clambering into the shaft. The effect on Robin is dramatic. She quadruples the speed at which she is dragging herself along. She jinks left, then right, in an effort to put as much distance between her and her pursuer. In the distance, she hears an angry male voice complain he is stuck followed by a stream of invective from Gates.

Good. Sometimes it pays to be born small.

Robin continues her escape, hardly feeling the stabs of pain from the bruising on her hands and knees. After wriggling and sliding for as long as she can bear, she halts her escape and tries to get her bearings. She can see a larger ventilation grate ahead in the shaft and she slithers up to it and looks down. She gasps.

In the best quality light since the ER room, Robin peers down into what looks like a huge control room full of knobs and dials. It resembles a power station she once visited on holiday in America which ran from a hydro-electric dam near Paige at the head of the Colorado River, Arizona.

Thinking there might a way of communicating with the outside world, Robin unscrews the grate with her one remaining coin. She drops lightly through the vent onto the top of a cabinet. It's next to the long array of dials which take up half the enormous room.

Bathed in blue light, the room feels cold and sinister. With no clue what the instruments covering the control desk are for, Robin makes her way along the length of it looking for something she might recognise which will provide a clue to the room's use.

None of it makes any sense to her apart from a large red LED display in the centre of the console which reads 'HAARP Tesla Technical Array Power Level Maximum Level'. She remembers the video of Michael's interrogation where he talked about HAARP.

So he did know.

But why would Gates and his goons be prepared to kill over it? Whatever this place is, there is no way it is being sanctioned at government level. This is a renegade project. It must be. But how can this place be still functioning when all the power is off? Maybe that's what's causing the power loss in the first place?

Then Robin finds a laptop at the far end of the desk. It is already powered up and seems to be functioning. Trying to steady her hands, Robin starts to log into her webmail account. She's in! She glances nervously over her shoulder and waits for the software to load.

"Come on, come on," she mutters anxiously to herself.

Her account pops up and she immediately opens a new email and types "manley.naswell@defense.gov" into the address bar.

"Let's find out if they know what's going down here at the US Defense Department."

But the door crashes open before she has a chance to type the email. Gates and the soldiers are in the room. Robin is running as fast as she can back along the control console.

"Stop or I shoot!" Gates yells.

Robin is not stopping for anyone, least of all a psycho like Gates. She leaps up onto the desk and makes for the open ventilation grille.

"Shoot the bitch," shouts Gates and the soldiers draw a bead on Robin and open fire.

Bullets slam into the plaster behind her disappearing feet and then they trace a path after her in the ventilation shaft as she wriggles away as fast as she can. As each bullet penetrates the metal a pencil-thin beam from the light below punches into the darkness of the shaft.

Robin realises there is something dark and warm running down her neck and dripping onto the cold metal of the box-shaped shaft. She puts her hand up to her ear and she feels warm sticky blood trickling from the side of her head. One of the bullets has grazed her left temple—another half inch to the right and she would have been killed.

Although it's bleeding quite freely, it feels superficial to her. Lucky girl. She wriggles faster and the fading sound of the automatic fire becomes sporadic then stops. Robin becomes conscious of the burning ache from her hands and knees from crawling so far on the unforgiving, cold surface of the air-conditoning shafts. Cuts and grazes criss-cross her palms and the knees of her jeans are shredded.

Eventually she stops crawling, secure in the knowledge her assailants can't follow her and she is safe for the time being.

Exhausted, she curls up and falls asleep almost immediately.

🎵🎵🎵

Gates is pacing around the swimming pool in the near darkness. A standard issue army sidearm is gripped loosely in his right palm. He hefts the Beretta M9A1 into the fire position occasionally and sights down the laser mounted on the rail along the top of the barrel.

He lets the red pinprick of light from the laser rest on doors, hand rails, and the mirror-like surface of the water as if he is hoping to see something which isn't there.

Then a gentle intermittent "plip-plop" becomes audible. Gates swings the laser beam around until he identifies the cause of the dripping. He can just make out something black spreading in a slick on the surface of the murky, dark water. He turns on his pocket flashlight and illuminates the area. As he thought, blood.

From the ventilation shaft above the pool.

Robin is shaken out of sleep by the violent and deafening explosion from the bullet which misses her by less than six inches. She screams in fright involuntarily and jerks bolt upright.

"Are you coming down or will I have to shoot you where you are? Makes no odds." Gates voice, though muffled, is clear enough in the shaft.

There is a pause, and then the ventilator grille through which Robin's blood had been dripping, falls into the water. Robin's slim body lowers into view. She hesitates while she assesses the drop, then she splashes into the water and swims slowly to the edge.

Gates, grinning evilly from ear to ear, remains crouched and ready to shoot. He makes no move to help Robin drag herself in her soaked clothes out of the chilly water.

"Well look what we have here. You really have been a monumental pain in the ass." Gates almost spits the words out.

Robin notices that she can see dawn breaking through a window. A window! The pool must be built into the side of the hill the castle sits on. The first red rays of daylight are spreading across the miles of heather outside. It looks quite beautiful, reflects Robin.

"Get out and consider yourself under arrest. If you try to run I will shoot you," snarls Gates. He has the red laser pinpoint of the Beretta in the middle of her forehead.

"I'm too tired to run anymore," shrugs Robin. Her arms are spread on the poolside but she can't muster the energy to drag herself out.

Then, from somewhere behind Robin, there is a deep, animalistic growl. The sound of a powerful and deadly beast. The sound of death. Gates spins round and waves the bright white beam of his flashlight around, looking for the source of the chilling sound.

"Someone let loose a black panther?" asks Gates.

"Much worse," replies Robin. It's all she can say between her chattering teeth, which is more of a reaction to hearing the sound again than the cold. "That's the thing which attacked Eli."

There is another longer, lower growl which continues to rumble as the first rays of dawn break over the surface of the pool. It stops as abruptly as it started as the red pool of scintillating light spreads wider and wider. Captive and captor wait motionless and silent for it to recommence, but it doesn't. They are alone again.

The lights come on, bathing the pool room in an unfamiliar harsh glare.

"Whatever it is has gone," announces Gates. "Now move. You and I need to have a little chat."

He motions with the gun for Robin to get out, which she does reluctantly. She battles to hold back tears of fear and exhaustion. But she would rather die than let Gates see her crumble.

Locked in a cell with Gates and no one else, Robin feels more scared than at any other point in the preceding forty eight hours. Wordlessly, Gates lashes her hands together and suspends her roughly from an overhead beam.

Her feet barely make contact with the floor and her already-sore wrists start to hurt badly almost immediately from the weight of her own body. To relieve the pressure on her wrists she needs to stand on tip-toe. Within a few seconds her feet start to cramp and she relaxes her tippy-toe ballerina stance and transfers the strain to her wrists. Gates watches her dispassionately.

"I need to know a few things before I throw you in with the others," he says flatly.

"So they are still alive?" she asks, fishing for information. For anything she can use to regain an advantage.

"I didn't say that," he replies. "Tell me what you saw before you escaped."

"I don't know what you mean," she replies through the increasing pain.

"Oh you do, you do." Gates, unbelievably, is uncoiling his belt and starting to wrap the opposite end to the buckle around his fist.

"What are you going to do with that?" asks Robin accusingly as she stares at the cruel-looking buckle.

Gates circles her slowly and menacingly.

"Nothing if you tell me what I want to know. What did you see when you were spying on me? What were you trying to send to your friend who works at the Defense Department?"

"I am from Palestine. I've met your sort before and you don't frighten me," she says, trying to sound braver than she feels.

Wordlessly, Gates steps in and rips off her t-shirt with both hands exposing her naked breasts. Robin stifles a sob and spins on her restraints in an attempt to shrink away from him.

"We'll see about that," Gates says as he tightens the belt around his knuckles.

He steps back, swings the leather belt and the buckle hits Robin in the middle of her shoulders. A red hot lance of pain shoots through her body as if she has been electrified. She bites down to suppress a scream.

"Still feeling brave? Tell me what I need to know and we'll stop."

Robin remains stubbornly mute. Tears involuntarily spring from her eyes and run down her dirty face, mixing with the dried blood from the head wound.

"No?"

Gates takes a step back and strikes her again with another stinging blow. Robin almost faints and slumps in the bindings. Her blood supply has been cut off at the wrists. Pins and needles have given way to numbness which deadens the pain.

He whips her and then she can hear the hiss of the

leather as it approaches yet again. She loses count of the blows after six as they merge into one sea of pain which mercifully she begins to sink into.

Blackness.

A blurry face is floating in front of her. Gates? Robin tries to blink but her eyes feel glued half-shut. A voice is speaking to her.

"Robin? Robin? For Christ's sake what has that butchering maniac done to you?"

Robin tries to speak but her mouth feels as gummed up as her eyes.

A gentle hand is wiping her face with something wet. The glue is being cleaned away and she is able to blink. She moves her jaw which hurts a lot. Maybe it's broken?

As the blood and dirt is wiped away, Robin is able to focus better and the face before her becomes more discernible until she can make out it is Trent. The combination of fear and disgust on his face scares her.

"How bad is it?" she asks shakily.

"Bad," Trent replies quietly.

The pain from the belt lashes competes with the burning from where the bullet grazed the side of her head and the acute lightning bolts from her jaw. He must have hit me as well she thinks dully.

Trent is visibly shaken by the state Robin is in and he does his best to make her comfortable. She commits a major mistake by leaning back and trying to lie down but the incredible waves of agony which course through her body immediately propel her to roll gingerly onto her front, helped by Trent, and she uses his jacket as a pillow.

It's then she notices Gareth in his wheelchair watching her with compassionate eyes.

"Hey," she manages to grunt.

"Hey back," intones Gareth in his signature monotone synthesised voice.

Robin holds Gareth's gaze until her eyes start to shut again and she is overcome with exhaustion.

"She's sleeping," Trent tells Gareth.

They sit in silence in the cell. Unspoken words hang heavy in the air between them. Despite his attempts to clean her up as best he can, Robin looks like a car crash victim still waiting for a paramedic.

The door opens abruptly. Rachel and Michael are pushed at gunpoint by the soldiers into the same cell as Trent and the others.

"You woke up," observes Gareth.

Michael is helping steady Rachel, who appears disorientated and dazed. Trent looks at the way Michael is with Rachel and decides he doesn't like what he sees. Instead of going to comfort his wife, he stays seated next to Robin.

Rachel takes in how badly-injured Robin is and she puts a hand up to her mouth in horror.

"Oh my God, what's happened?"

Trent stands and goes to the cell door. He bangs on the glass and shouts at the guards, "We need help in here. This woman is going to die unless she receives urgent medical help."

The soldiers outside the cell ignore him but he persists and keeps banging his fist on the glass panel. "Hey, you. Get Gates. This woman is going to die and her blood will be on his hands!"

He continues his pounding.

"Trent, that's enough. They aren't interested," Rachel puts her hand on his shoulder gently.

Trent pushes it away and turns on her.

"Don't you dare tell me when it's enough. You were left in charge of caring for Eli and as far as I can see you fell asleep and he died."

Rachel starts to cry and Michael puts a consoling hand on her arm.

"And keep your hands off my wife," Trent snarls at Michael. The hand doesn't withdraw.

"No."

Michael shakes his head slowly and smiles at Trent in the way men can make a smile a taunt.

"It's time you had a reality check, Trent."

With an angry growl, Trent hurls himself at Michael. Trent is over six feet tall and well-built but Michael displays an animal grace as he sidesteps Trent and drives his elbow into the back of his head as Trent charges at him.

Trent yells in fury and pain as he lands face first in the corner of the cell. He's back on his feet in a second and charging at Michael for a second time. Rachel screams for them to stop and tries to get between them but is crushed as the two men charge each other like bulls. The three of them collapse to the ground in a whirling blur of arms and legs as Trent and Michael try to get at each other.

In the melee, Trent lands a blow accidentally to Rachel's jaw and she crashes backwards against the cell door. The impact finally attracts the attention of the guards who glance through the glass inspection hatch and then are gone.

Rachel tries to rise unsteadily to her feet but is too dazed already before getting involved in the fight to be in full command of her motor functions.

"Dad, please stop!" intones Gareth dispassionately, belying the confused emotions he is experiencing.

Michael is the first person he has met in a long time that he trusts and genuinely likes. He has developed a healthy male competition with his father but after everything they have been through together, he feels fiercely protective of him and the sight of his father exchanging blows with his recently-acquired friend is too much to stand.

He drives his wheelchair between them in lieu of knowing what else to do. His physical intervention breaks the spell of mutually assured destruction and the two assailants finally stop fighting.

At this moment, the lock rattles in the door and Gates enters the room. He is followed by two of the armed soldiers, their lightweight Belgian-designed Herstal M17 assault rifles raised in readiness. Trent has grown up around weapons and knows the rifles being pointed at them carry a high velocity 7.62 mm round which at close range could penetrate and kill two people.

"Put your hands up," Gates orders. "Both of you."

Michael reluctantly does as he is bidden and slowly raises his big boxer's hands. Gareth notes Michael is not even breathing hard, unlike his father who is gasping for breath.

Gates looks around slowly at each of their faces, as if he is trying to decide who to shoot first. His eyes finally linger on the prone, broken little form of Robin who looks terrible.

"Were you fighting over her or her?" He cocks his head at Robin then at Rachel, who also has her hands raised in surrender.

"Neither," Michael interjects. "We just don't like

each other."

"The one over there does look like she needs some attention." Gates concludes.

"Her over there, the woman you almost beat to death, is called Robin," pants Trent. "And if we don't do something, she may die from shock apart from anything else. What kind of sadistic, psychopathic maniac are you anyway?"

Gates shrugs non-comittally.

"We all choose our own path. She chose to evade being detained and took the path of a fugitive. In the process she gained access to a secure area and needed to be taught a lesson."

"Some kind of lesson," snorts Trent in disgust.

"I wouldn't expect a joke like you to understand real discipline or high stakeholder expectations," states Gates flatly.

"You know nothing about me," counters Trent.

"Oh but I do," says Gates mysteriously. "Much as I'd love to provide you with the details about your failed military career to prove that fact, we need to do something about your disobedient friend there," he continues with finality.

On Gates's instruction, two of the soldiers shoulder their firearms and pick Robin up and carry her out.

"Where are you going?" asks Trent to Gates's disappearing back.

"To the ER. I suggest you and the kid come with me and you leave your boyfriend and your lady wife here. And put your arms down, you look ridiculous."

They drop their arms. Trent and Gareth follow Robin, leaving Michael and Rachel locked in the cell by the soldiers.

In the ER, Robin is laid on the same cot where Eli

died two hours ago. Gareth takes up position as close to the cot as the soldiers will allow him. Trent breaks open a syringe and takes some blood from Robin's arm. She comes round as he withdraws the needle.

She looks at Trent with bleary, unfocussed eyes and asks an imploring question with her bloodshot eyes. Trent catches the look and shakes his head imperceptibly. He places a few drops of blood in an analyser and waits for it to give him her blood type. O Negative blips up on the small LED screen after ten seconds.

"I need O Negative," he says to the silent soldiers.

"That's a nuisance," says Gates, seeming genuinely annoyed. "There isn't any. Too rare a blood type I imagine."

Gareth looks at his father who mouths "No" at him.

"I'm O Negative," Gareth says with his usual talent for understatement.

A few minutes later Gareth is attached to a plastic tube and a red line of blood is dripping into a donor bag attached to the arm of his wheelchair.

"This is a bad idea, Gareth. You know how anaemic you are."

Trent stands over his son looking worried as well as terribly grey from exhaustion. The events of the last forty eight hours have taken a drastic toll on him.

"We don't have a choice." Gareth is looking at Robin. She is still unconscious.

# Rachel

Rachel and Michael sit next to one another on the drop-down bunk bed in the cell. It is a very rudimentary thing supported by chains. A thin foam mattress no more than an inch deep is covered by a rough wool blanket. Rachel focusses on the hard metal lip of the bunk as it cuts into her thighs.

Michael puts a comforting arm around her shoulders and she doesn't remove it. She realises she quite likes the comforting feel of it. Rachel thinks about how long it's been since Trent did the same thing, when it wasn't just an unsubtle prelude to sex.

"You OK?" asks Michael. She turns and looks into his impossibly deep blue eyes.

"No," she admits.

Another first, recognising she is anything but a solid, immoveable rock. She thinks how cathartic it is to stop pretending to be bullet-proof just for a moment.

"Do you mind me putting my arm around you?" asks Michael gently.

"No. It's nice. And I need something to hang on-to."

They continue to sit. Rachel tries to remember the last time she didn't feel the need to be strong for someone. If it wasn't Trent, it was Gareth. Not their fault, either of them, but they were both so needy in their own way. There hadn't been a moment since she gave up modelling and took her behavioural therapy masters so she could look after her declining, traumatised husband when she had let guard down. But now it was happening with this tall, handsome, blonde-haired stranger who had showed her nothing but kindness and consideration from the beginning.

The first gentleman she has encountered in a long time. And he smells so good too, which men rarely do. He has this incredible aura around him of apples and fresh air the whole time. It must be his pheromones, she thinks. Rachel turns and tilts her head up slightly to look at Michael properly. He isn't fazed by this and he returns her gaze steadily without seeming to blink.

"Why was I asleep?" she asks him, looking deep into his blue eyes.

"You needed to be protected," he replies simply.

"I had a dream where I was surrounded by beautiful angels. There was one in a gorgeous robe edged with red and gold."

Michael nods in recognition.

"That was Archangel Metatron."

"Who? He sounds like a Power Ranger."

"Metatron is the most powerful and important angel. He stands guard over the stellar gateway, the bridge to heaven."

Rachel takes Michael's hand in hers and stares into his eyes.

"Did I almost die then? All I did was fall asleep."

Michael covers her long, slender hand with his and draws imperceptibly closer to her.

"You needed to be as far away as possible. You had a choice to make."

Without another word his lips brush hers and he withdraws slightly to assess her reaction. She doesn't move a muscle but her eyes dart from his eyes to his lips and back to his eyes again. He kisses her gently and her coral-pink lips open involuntarily to receive his tongue.

"I'm having trouble getting a line in."

Trent flicks Robin's arm a few times until a vein raises itself and he slides the needle in and secures it with a plaster.

"There. Got it." He allows himself a tiny smile.

The crash cart starts pinging and when Trent glances up he sees it is flashing 'Tachycardic'—which he knows means her heart has stopped. The display shows her blood gases—the amount of dissolved oxygen in her blood keeping her alive—have dropped to a dangerously low eighty-five percent.

Robin's face is white beneath the dried blood and her lips are blue. Trent gives her CPR by alternately pinching her nostrils and blowing into her mouth and then pushing down on her chest rhythmically while he counts.

Gates is hovering, more curious than concerned.

Trent leans close to Gates's ear out of Gareth's range and whispers hoarsely, "Look Gates. I know you intend to kill us all eventually but help me at least try to save Robin right now. Get me some Atropine. Now."

Gates returns his stare and for a moment does nothing. Then he makes a decision and reaches into one of the glass-fronted cabinets. He withdraws his hand and places a large metal syringe in Trent's outstretched hand.

Trent turns to Robin and places two fingers on her motionless chest to orientate himself to the position of her heart. Satisfied, he rams the syringe into her where he hopes her stopped heart is and depresses the plunger in one quick motion.

The result is instant. Robin gasps as her heart restarts suddenly and she gulps in air as her cardiovascular system lurches violently into action. The blood gas readings start to climb immediately past ninety and upwards. The colour returns to her face and her lips become a normal reddish hue once again.

Robin's eyes open and she finds Trent's face. She lifts one hand and squeezes his although she is very weak. Then her eyes close and she slips into oblivion once again.

Rachel is totally confused by the conflicting emotions racing through her mind. And the feelings coursing through her body like lightning bolts. Her husband is probably only a few metres away from the cell where she is running her fingers through the thick blonde hair of the most angelic man she has ever met. She realises she has been aching to stroke Michael's silky hair and feel his lips on hers ever since they first met.

Suddenly all her focus is on needing him close, to hold her, to feel his warmth, have his taut skin next to hers. She has never in her life felt an overpowering lust like this. Her breasts are aching and she is throbbing between her legs as she becomes engorged and wet in anticipation.

Michael doesn't say anything and behaves as if they are completely alone ... the image comes into Rachel's mind of being on a desert island somewhere with the warm ocean lapping at their feet and the soft white sand supporting the curve of their bodies. Weirdly, she can hear the sound of the ocean now, of tropical birds calling above her head and the breeze teasing her long dark brown hair. The dank cell has almost disappeared out of her peripheral vision and she feels completely safe, warm and receptive to Michael.

Rachel realises she has her hand on Michael's arm and can feel the finely-contoured muscles of his body as they bunch and flex at her touch. He is kissing her gently on the lips, her eyelids and along the line of her collarbone. He caresses her back smoothly and slowly with his strong, warm hands.

The thought that she has never wanted, never *needed* a man inside her so urgently doesn't even shock her.

It's as if everything no longer matters or has substance. Trent in his constantly angry state, Gareth's pleading eyes and fragility, the trauma of the last two days. All gone. Maybe she did die and this is now the afterlife. Anyway, she doesn't care anymore. About anything. Except for right here and right now.

Does that make me a slut? she wonders to herself. I don't care if it does as nothing matters now. I just have to have this gorgeous man, this beautiful thing, inside me.

And then he is. She is shocked by the unexpected coolness of his cock. As it slides deeper into her with incredible gentleness, she is aroused beyond comprehension by its girth and incredible rigidity. The feeling of wholeness, completeness, is overpowering. Within a few long, rhythmic strokes, Rachel can feel the somersaulting butterflies and muscular tightening of an orgasm building within her.

When she comes it is like nothing she has ever experienced. A wave of joyous pleasure, which feels so right and so wonderful, crashes over her. She is only dimly aware of how she clutches and scratches at Michael's broad, muscular back and squeezes his thighs with her shimmering legs.

Her orgasm goes on and on. She feels like she is exploding. As the sensation is subsiding, along comes a second wave and it bursts over her once again. She senses Michael's beautiful, magical penis thicken even more at the base where it is engaging with her clitoris and an enormous gush of semen is ejected deep into her womb.

Never has someone come so deep inside her. The rush of liquid shooting up into her triggers a third, seismically-profound, orgasm.

Once it finally subsides she hugs Michael so tightly he can't breathe. She is still holding her breath, which she finally expels in an enormous sob and starts to shudder uncontrollably with spent emotion.

"Oh my God, that was unbelievable."

She releases the seven foot tall giant and clasps his handsome face with her long fingers.

"That was the most incredible thing I have ever experienced."

They draw apart slightly, still panting hard. The beach and the water have disappeared. Rachel can feel the rough material of the blanket beneath her again and the cold metal edge of the cot.

Michael looks deeply into her eyes.

"You are the most beautiful woman I have ever met. But this needs to be our secret and it can never happen again."

Rachel takes this in but rebels against his request.

"I'll leave Trent for you. I'll do anything. I have to have that again."

Michael moves away and starts buttoning himself

up.

"It can't happen Rachel. It was a moment but I don't want to ruin your life as well as two others."

"You can't do that to a woman and then call it a day. That is going to be impossible for me. You can't have a conscious all of a sudden."

"Listen to yourself. It was incredible for me too but it's a mistake. We have no future. I'm sorry," Michael says gently.

"Well it's a bit late for that Michael." Rachel tucks her blouse back into her jeans and zips them up.

The cell door opens.

Trent stumbles as he is pushed into the room by the guards, followed by Gareth whirring along in his wheel-chair. Trent is too distracted to notice the pair's close-ness or how dishevelled and wanton his wife looks.

Rachel looks up.

"Where's Robin?"

Trent has disintegrated since he left for the ER. His hands are shaking and he looks wild and unravelled.

"Still in ER. That bastard almost killed her," he re-plies, trembling.

Gareth is giving Michael his stare. He has read the situation correctly but only his eyes can give away the churning emotion he is experiencing. Gareth watches Michael's face carefully.

Michael avoids looking directly at Gareth but he knows he is being scrutinised. He touches Rachel gently on the arm, making Gareth's eyes narrow slightly in un-spoken anger.

"Rachel why don't you ask them to let you see your friend?" he asks quietly.

Trent bangs his fist on the glass panel in the door once again and beckons one of the soldiers over.

"Open up soldier. My wife would like to see her friend."

The soldier hesitates, looking at Trent's unsteady features.

"Open up. Christ, it's not like we have anywhere to go!"

The soldier clangs open the door and lets Rachel past him.

"You taking her?" he asks Trent.

"Do you want me to go with her dad?" Gareth asks levelly.

Trent looks round at his son as if has just noticed him for the first time and shakes his head hesitatingly.

"No, I'll go. Thanks Gareth. You stay here with Michael."

The cell door bangs shut behind them, leaving an uncomfortable silence hanging in the air between Gareth and Michael. Rotating his wheelchair one hundred and eighty degrees on its axis, a manoeuvre he has perfected since they became trapped in the castle, Gareth locks eyes with Michael.

"So." Gareth says just one word.

"So," Michael acknowledges as he compresses his mouth into a defensive crimp.

"I know what you did," intones Gareth.

"What did I do Gareth?" asks Michael innocently.

"You know. Are you trying to destroy us all? I looked up to you. I thought you had more principles than that."

"I don't know what you're talking about Gareth. I really don't."

Michael's poker face unsettles Gareth and he wonders if maybe he is mistaken after all. Well, only one way to find out, he thinks to himself.

Two soldiers stand guard in the ER. For a second time, Rachel gasps when she sees little Robin lying drugged and unconscious on the same cot where Eli died not long ago. Robin looks even worse than in the cell as the bruises have had time to form.

Rachel puts her hand up to her mouth in horror as she gazes at the contusions and discoloured bruises across Robin's back and the red, swollen puffiness around her eyes, one of which is almost completely closed due to the swelling. The yellowing bruises on Robin's jaw where Gates punched her after she lost consciousness are vivid.

"What kind of an evil maniac is he?" wonders Rachel out loud.

Trent mutters shakily, "I had to inject Atropine into her heart to save her. She stopped breathing. No time for paddles. I almost lost her. Another one..." His voice trails off.

"Almost lost another one what Trent?" Gates has appeared silently behind them, unnoticed.

Rachel turns to him and stares with disbelief at Gates's impassive face.

"Do you not feel even the slightest twinge of remorse, Gates?"

"I ran Guantanamo for five years. This is nothing. She'll be OK."

"Well that explains a lot," shrugs Rachel.

"You don't like losing your little soldier girls do you, Trent? As I said, I've been reading your file."

Gates allows himself a fleeting smile of satisfaction.

"Your female co-pilot was captured by the Taliban after the crash apparently. They do despicable things to the women, far worse than the men."

Rachel looks aghast at her husband who is visibly caving before her.

"Is that true, Trent? You said the co-pilot was killed in the crash."

Trent stares at the floor then his shoulders begin to heave.

"I'm afraid lied. I lied to you. I couldn't bear to admit it."

He starts to sob quietly.

Then he says in a whisper, "They raped her and staked her out naked in the sun. The dogs got her."

"It was not a quick death," Gates adds helpfully. "They were drawn by the scent of blood and started on the area where the blood was coming from first. They ate her from the inside out as it were."

"But how do you know this?" Rachel asks Gates in disbelief.

"Eli led the attempt to save her after he stopped the same band from taking me when I was trapped in the wreckage of the crash. He found her. It took him five years to tell me but he had to report it."

Trent's voice is a monotone and hardly more than a croak.

Rachel touches Trent's face gently with the back of her hand and strokes his cheek.

"You poor angel. Is there no end to this?"

Trent clasps his palm round her hand and embraces her while tears stream down his grimy face.

"Oh please. Show some grit Colonel."

It's the first time Gates has used his official rank, Trent dimly registers. He's got my file. I wonder what else he knows?

Trent and Rachel are pushed unceremoniously back into the cell by the soldiers. Michael and Gareth haven't moved since they left.

"You're all just reincarnated Nazis," drones Gareth ineffectually at the grunts. It's impossible to be cutting when your comments are stripped of any emotion.

The four of them sit in dejected silence for a while. Gareth is staring at Rachel. She feels the intensity of his gaze and looks up.

"Why are you staring at me, Gareth? I've told you before how unnerving it is when you do that."

"How many more Rachel?" is the flat question from Gareth.

Rachel looks blank.

"Excuse me?"

Gareth is not going to be diverted.

"How many men have you slept with since you took my mother's place?"

Trent, despite his dazed state, registers the jibe.

"Gareth, what's got into you? How dare you accuse Rachel at a time like this?"

"Dad I love you but we need to talk about this. Rachel sleeps with other men behind your back."

Michael lies back on the cot and stares at the ceiling. He doesn't want to be part of this.

"How dare you Gareth? After everything I've done for you!" Rachel's tone is even but there is a barely-concealed edge to her voice.

"You are a whore," states Gareth flatly.

Michael can't hold his tongue any longer.

"That's enough you little shit."

Trent straightens up.

"Stay out of this Michael," he warns.

Michael runs his thick, strong fingers through his

luxurious blonde hair and his deep blue eyes flash with anger and something else Trent can't quite reach.

"Oh I don't think he can," grates Gareth. "You're in deep aren't you Michael?"

"That's enough, Gareth."

Rachel has shrunk into the corner of the cell and her arms are folded defensively.

"I don't want to hear any more from you Gareth. This situation is getting to us all."

Trent sinks back on the cot. He looks defeated.

An awkward silence descends on the cell.

Rachel is lying on her back on the second cot staring at the ceiling. Gates has removed all their personal possessions, including her watch, so she has lost all track of time. The bare bulb hanging down in the middle of the makeshift cell is lit so she assumes it's still daytime based on the nightly power failures which rob them of all electrical power. She tries to relax enough to sleep but it evades her efforts to slip into dreams for just a few minutes to escape the living horror they are in.

She wonders if Gates plans to kill them all now or later. One at a time or individually? What does a sadistic sociopath do to get the most pleasure from seeing other's suffer? Killing us one at a time seems the most likely option, she thinks gloomily.

She notices a large black cockroach scuttling across the bare concrete floor.

"What would you do?" she asks the cockroach out loud. "How would you escape from here?"

To her astonishment, the creature stops and turns its scaly face to hers and says: "I'd stop feeling sorry for myself, then I would do what I am bidden by Lucifer."

Rachel blinks and shakes her head. Did a cockroach just say something or was it in her head? When she looks again it's gone. There is just a bare concrete floor.

Suddenly a sharp pain runs up her left side like electricity, then again up her right side. The pain quickly moves to her stomach area and she cries out loud. She looks around for the others but she is alone. They must have asked to check on Robin while she slept. They'll be back in a moment and she'll be OK she decides.

The pain doubles in intensity and she moans. She doubles up and clutches her belly with both hands. She is going to have to get help. It must be appendicitis or food poisoning, not that she's eaten anything for 12 hours. Where is everyone? She calls for help.

As the spasms increase intensely, her calls become screams. Rachel is really frightened now. She feels like she is going to die. Maybe that's it. Gates has poisoned her to satisfy his twisted appetite for suffering and fear. He seems to live off fear. It makes him strong. He is the modern world she thinks. A cancerous tumour growing stronger by feeding on fear and anger.

Suddenly she can see with clarity what is going wrong with the whole world. The terrifying experiences over the last few days are like normal life but with the volume turned up. We are all scared of something, mainly ourselves. This castle is my body, my mind, my life and it is dying of fear. It's poisoning me and unless I'm very careful it's going to kill me.

"Jesus that hurts," she exclaims.

Then Michael is beside her. He holds her hand and strokes her brow. When Michael withdraws his hand it is wet from her sweat.

"Michael, what's happening to me?" she struggles

to ask between ragged breaths.

"Shhh darling. It's OK. You're having a baby," he replies matter of factly.

"What? That's impossible. That's what Ted thought. But I'm not even pregnant!" she gasps.

"Breathe, breathe. You are having a baby. Our baby," he says in a soothing voice.

"Where's my husband?" she hisses between clenched teeth.

"You don't need him anymore. You've got me," he replies.

Then the pain increases once again to a level that Rachel could never have imagined. She lets out a long low scream which rises in pitch until she feels like she is tearing out her own vocal chords. She feels something enormous give and there is a wet gush from between her legs. Michael is crouched on the floor in front of her and he raises himself up, very slowly. He has something in his arms which he is cradling gently.

She cranes her head round to see what it is and her world stops dead. The deformed creature in his arms is horrible. It has no eyes or ears. Just a distended mouth which has been crudely stitched up with something which looks like a thick shoelace. It isn't moving.

Michael is crying.

"What's that.. thing?" she asks.

"It's your baby darling. The baby Lucifer."

He tries to hand her the frightening twisted bundle but she pushes it away in disgust.

"But he's dead. And you killed him."

Rachel sits bolt upright. The cell is dark and the others are all sleeping. There is no baby. Michael's chest rises and falls slowly where he lies on the cot. She slips over to where he is sleeping and shakes him.

His cobalt blue eyes flick open as he if had been wide awake the entire time. She places her fingers on his lips and sinks her nails into his arm with her other hand. He doesn't react to the sensation at all. He just looks evenly into her eyes.

"I just had a dream." she whispers as quietly as she can despite her agitated state.

"A bad one by the look of you," he observes, whispering back.

"Who or what are you Michael? You still haven't explained that to me despite the fact I've asked you twice," she almost hisses at him.

"Didn't Jesus ask Judas three times? I'm an activist. I came here to take this place down before they destroy everything."

"That's why you're here. But who the fuck are you? And what's it got to do with Judas."

Michael hesitates as he stares into both her eyes intermittently. His gaze flicks to and fro urgently between her beautiful hazel eyes as if he is trying to see into her soul.

"You've asked me three times. Like Jesus asked Judas if he would betray him."

Michael sees the blank, uncomprehending look on Rachel's face.

"Never mind. Look, do you think you can handle the truth?"

"I don't have a choice do I."

Michael pauses and takes a deep breath.

"I am an angel. An archangel in fact."

He waits for the statement to sink in.

Rachel looks bemused then hurt.

"Don't tease me. I'm serious."

"So am I. I am Archangel Michael. I chose to incarnate to understand what it is to be human. We angels envy the gift of life you have. I wanted to meet someone like you but you had to come to me as my passage is limited. I am stuck here."

"Oh come on. Am I still dreaming? Please don't lie to me, it's pathetic."

"I asked you if you could handle the truth and that is the truth. I swear."

Rachel leans back and slumps down dejectedly.

"If I can't believe you, who or what can I believe?"

Michael turns onto his side and cups her face in his big hands.

"You can trust me. I love you."

Rachel melts and very slowly she leans into him and looks at his soft, almost feminine lips and then into his deep blue eyes. She kisses him very lightly, hesitates, and then kisses him again with urgency. Michael sighs and sinks his strong, square fingers into the long, loose auburn hair which hangs in coils down her back.

A blur of motion flashes past the corner of her eye and Michael's head snaps back. A blow lands in his face and his lip sprays a fine mist of blood as he disappears. Trent is already sitting on his chest as they land heavily on the concrete floor raining blows down on his face and chest.

Trent snarls like an animal as he punches Michael repeatedly in the face. Michael drags his long arms up to protect himself and heaves Trent off his chest to get the upper hand.

He pins Trent's arms back and lands a good, hard blow square in his face. Rachel is suddenly between them flailing her arms and screaming. Trent instinctively raises a fist to protect himself and strikes Rachel hard on the side of her face. She rocks back and hits her head on the unrelenting concrete floor with an audible crack.

"Rachel!" he shouts, horrified.

Michael lands another crunching blow in his face and they roll away from Rachel together, still locked in what looks like a fight to the death. All Trent's suspicion and resentment spills out and mixes with the splashes of blood landing in thick gobs on the floor.

Gareth has been watching the fight from the corner. Tears stream down his expressionless face and his eyes are like saucers.

"Stop. Please stop. You're going to kill my dad."

The two battling men collapse to the floor fighting for breath, the spell of destruction broken. Gareth, his movement restricted by the charging plug attached to a wall socket, whirrs a few feet nearer Rachel, who lies motionless.

"Rachel? Rachel? Are you dead?" he asks insistently in his woefully inadequate flat drone. She doesn't respond.

Then Trent is at his side. He bends down and gently lifts his wife from the floor and lays her down again on one of the cots. He checks her vital signs.

"I think she's ok. She's out at the moment."

He strokes her forehead and watches her eyes for signs of movement. While Trent keeps a vigil over Rachel as he waits for her to come round, Gareth notices Michael is crouching on his haunches on the cot and stroking his arms as if smoothing imaginary feathers like a bird.

He reminds Gareth of the evil gargoyle over the entrance to the hall. The entrance. Gareth starts thinking about the first moment he saw the castle and noticed the gargoyle with its protruding tongue. Michael has his chin in his hands watching Trent with Rachel.

"Is she going to be OK?" he asks.

Trent turns to Michael. He has regained a little of his Alpha Male essence.

"I don't want to see you near her again. Stay away from her. Is that clear?"

Michael uncoils himself and stands up to his full, towering seven feet in height.

"Doesn't Rachel have a say in this?" he asks slowly.

Trent looks at him levelly, understanding something in the dynamic between them has altered now the dirty secret is out.

"Right now Rachel has fallen under your spell and doesn't know what the fuck she's doing. So no, she doesn't. I speak for my wife and I want you to stay away and stop whatever bullshit mind-control you've got going on whatever it is. Are we clear?" Trent's jaw is set.

Michael says nothing. He studies Trent's face and his eyes defocus. Trent gets the feeling Michael is in his head, looking.

"Get OUT of my head you bastard!"

Trent is taken aback when he realises he has said it out loud. Michael smiles slowly and sits down on the cot again. He starts to whistle a short sequence of notes which Gareth recognises and it makes his blood run cold. The same sequence of notes the mysterious harp plays.

"What is that?" asks Gareth.

Michael smiles sweetly at him and keeps whistling the same sequence as the harp. Abruptly, he stops.

"You heard it too then?"

"We all did," replies Gareth in his flat monotone.

"What is doing it?" asks Trent suspiciously.

"Who knows?" Michael leans back on the cot and laces his broad hands behind his blonde halo of hair. "Who knows?" He repeats the question to no one in particular. "Maybe we'll find out before Gates kills us all."

Trent notices Rachel's eyelids flutter. "I think she's coming round," he says, relieved.

# HAARP

"I'm going to let you all in on the secret," Gates says conspiratorially.

They are assembled in the vault-like control room. Everyone, that is, apart from Robin who hasn't come round since Gates almost beat her to death. The four soldiers stand either side of Gates, their assault rifles slung over their shoulders with the muzzles pointed at the ground.

"Is this another of your perverted games Gates?" Michael asks.

"Why should it be? I'm going to level with you." Gates looks almost disappointed.

"What he means is, are you going to tell us some secrets just so you have an excuse to kill us all?" Trent asks.

"No one is going to kill anyone," lies Gates. "I thought as Michael and his cohorts went to all the effort to break in, the least I could do is tell him and the rest of you what it is you've stumbled on."

"Where are the other activists?" Gareth asks, half muffled by Trent and Michael standing in front of him.

"Sorry did the wheelchair say something?" asks Gates sarcastically.

With his beak of a nose and his peculiar curved chin, he looks more like a bird of prey than ever.

Gareth moves forward between Trent and Michael.

144

"I asked where the other activists are," repeats Gareth.

"Oh they're quite safe," replies Gates calmly.

"You killed two of my friends. Why should we trust anything you say?" asks Rachel.

Gates glares at Rachel. He is a woman-hater as well as a psychopath, Rachel concludes.

"Every time a woman addresses you Gates, you seem to go crazy," she observes.

"Oh don't worry, I loathe all of you equally. Although not as much as my dear government, for whom I reserve a special kind of bile."

"Because they don't want to be held responsible for wiping out the whole of the human race by any chance?" taunts Michael.

"They have no spine, any of them," snarls Gates. "The only ones who have any grit or resolve, are standing humbly before you in this room."

The implacable soldiers who stand beside Gates share a barely-noticeable smirk.

"All of us are wholly committed to what must be done."

"And what is so compelling that you are prepared to kill to achieve it?" Rachel asks quietly.

"I thought you'd never ask," beams Gates. "This facility is running a Tesla Technology Array."

"Is that what people refer to as HAARP? The High Frequency Active Auroral Programme?" interjects Michael.

"Yes it's the same thing," nods Gates. "But angels don't play this harp. I do."

"What does it do? We heard Michael talking about it but it's very confusing," interrupts Rachel.

"That's the wrong question. What doesn't it do

would be more appropriate," Gates replies. "The technology was discovered by a rather brilliant scientist called Nikola Tesla in the early part of the twentieth century. He found that it was possible to penetrate the ground, the upper atmosphere and the oceans with a certain kind of radio wave. But he only had access to very low power devices. Now we have beams which are one hundred thousand times more powerful than the most powerful radio station in the world."

"Radio? Doesn't sound very dangerous to me, "scoffs Rachel.

"Oh but it is," chides Gates. "We have the power to heat the very top of the earth's atmosphere in selected regions. This change in temperature makes the earth's atmosphere bulge upwards, dragging satellites we don't like out of orbit and making them crash back to earth. We also discovered these beams can pass messages through water which has never been possible before. By bouncing the beam off the atmosphere we can affect a region on the other side of the planet which is totally obscured by the curvature of the earth."

Gates waits for the impact of his words to sink in fully.

"Where my government and I parted company was the final stage of the story which is twofold. One, the incredible ability of the radio beam to change the path of the Jetstream by heating the atmosphere, resulting in drastic weather alterations and two, its potential for triggering major earthquakes and tsunami at will. We can deliver a tsunami against our enemies with many times the power of a conventional atomic bomb. We can make eight hundred miles of seabed suddenly rear up like an enraged demon and shake a country to bits. And the beauty of it is that it is, "he balls a fist into the palm of his hand with an explosive sound, "one hundred percent deniable. The perfect weapon."

Trent is horrified by what he has heard.

"But why? What does anyone have to gain?"

Gates looks triumphantly at Trent.

"That's easy. We can control the earth's weather and combat climate change, extend growing seasons and destroy our enemies who wish to harm us. And *you* are going to help me. In fact Trent, you are going to be my perfect deniability tool."

Trent shakes his head slowly.

"There is no way that is going to happen in this lifetime."

"That's where you are so wrong my friend. You are going to record a video stating you masterminded the whole idea and you will accept full responsibility. That's why you need to understand the whole picture."

"This place is already full of the bodies of people who have stood up to you and some who didn't even get the chance. You and I both know the same fate awaits us when you are done with us," replies Trent.

Gates stares levelly at Trent.

"You are going to admit liability on behalf of Israel for a HAARP attack on Iran which is going to trigger a 9.0 magnitude earthquake just off the coast of Iran very near the surface. The same intensity as Japan in fact. And a similar tsunami will be created which will surge over the coast of Iran for 30 miles, destroying sea defences and killing thousands. Iran's nuclear programme will be stopped for good and the country will be plunged into a civil war it will never recover from."

"I won't do that," states Trent.

"Oh but you will when you see your poor handicapped son swinging from a meat hook while I beat him to death," counters Gates conversationally.

They all look round instinctively for Gareth but he's nowhere to be seen.

"Find him!" shrieks Gates.

# Gareth

Gareth is making surprisingly good progress down the gravel road which leads away from the castle. The cool air blowing across the moors feels good on his face and he breathes a big lungful in. He moves as fast as the wheelchair will carry him at a stately four miles per hour.

He makes a quick mental calculation. His batteries have only just been fully recharged and have two hour's duration at full speed. It is probably only about six miles to the nearest houses outside Aviemore. Allowing for the route the road takes down the mountain which is not a straight line, it might be only eight miles in total. The same distance his chariot will take him before the battery dies. He might just make it.

The light is beginning to fade. Despite the shiver of fear that realisation causes to wash over him, he is excited and happy to have escaped unnoticed from the lunatic while he was giving the others their museum tour. Conscious he may be their last hope, he is buoyed by the pleasure of being free—however briefly.

A pair of crows circle low behind Gareth unnoticed.

Gareth crunches at a walking pace over the uneven gravel surface of the road away from the castle. It is going to be a long and difficult journey. The road is slightly rutted and not always flat. If I go over out here, he thinks ruefully, no one will ever find me. He has well and truly used up every one of his nine lives in the last two days. As he draws further away from the castle behind him, his sense of isolation and fear grows a knot of apprehension in his stomach. Because he is incapable of turning his head, he can't assess his progress although he knows it must be pretty glacial.

It is only a matter of minutes before they realise he has slipped away and they will be after him. He strains his ears over the whirr of the electric motor in the wheelchair and the crunch of the gravel beneath the wheels for the sound of the soldiers' boots or a car engine. They must have overcome the problem with dead electrics in the vehicles by now.

Nothing yet though and he's been on the road for more than ten minutes. It will be any time soon. Gareth feels his isolation and vulnerability in a sudden rush. He is a speck on the hillside and even tinier when he thinks about the chilly vastness of the Cairngorm mountains. Their mute grandeur stretches as far as he can see and he notices the approaching gloom is settling beautiful greys and purples across their peaks. The lavender and yellow of the highland heather in bloom paints a gorgeous tableau in swathes as far as the eye can see.

The natural beauty soothes the panic slightly as it builds a familiar rhythm in Gareth's chest. This is a test for me he thinks. Another mini-crucifixion in my bastard life to have to overcome. Maybe it will stop one day. I will find reason in all this shit which happens to me. So I killed my own mother and my twin brother. My father is a basket case and the woman he married to blot out the memory of his wife, my mother, has been having sex with a stranger right under his nose.

"Forgive her Gareth. Forgive yourself."

His mother's voice whispers in his ear as if carried on the mountain air currents which are whistling and dancing around him. Gareth feels tears start to form and the cold wind chills his cheeks as the tears run down his cheeks. A bus shelter is on his right for the bus which never seems to come. On the spur of the moment, he does a right turn so he is on the leeward side of the shelter out of the cold wind. The temporary respite is a relief.

Gareth reflects on what was, probably, just an imagined voice in his own head this time and about the nature of forgiveness. He had never trusted Rachel for the way she had moved in on his father. He was at least one generation older than her, maybe even two. What could a crumbling, confused man like his father offer her? Wasn't she an ex-model or something? She did have very long legs and supermodel hair so maybe that was right. He'd heard women saw men as projects for them to change, make better, manipulate.

Perhaps it was a little like buying a run-down house which had potential. Much more satisfying to make something your own. Yes he could see that. Was that the basis of attraction then? Weren't women drawn to men who could care for them, be the provider? Not much chance of that ever being true of me, Gareth thinks sadly to himself. I'm not stupid but there's no way I'm ever going to do something brilliant sitting in this milk float.

Maybe I could play the project card and find someone like Rachel myself who sees me as a challenge? Whoever she was, she would definitely need to be a girl who likes going on top anyway. They will always have their head turned by a fully-functioning guy though won't they? I would never be able to trust them. They would break my heart and there's nothing I could do to stop them. Like dad. He doesn't have any power anymore. He is as weak and vulnerable as me.

Can I forgive her for what she's done? She'll do it again won't she? She doesn't respect my father and she knows she can do what she wants. He should kill her really. No I shouldn't think things like that. It's wrong. And looked what happened to Eli and the others.

Thoughts become things.

Well if that's the case, I am going to think that Dad does have power. Rachel didn't mean it and I will forgive her for what she's done. Michael has a strange way of controlling people but he seems like a good person really. Consider how much he has helped us. He's looked out for me hasn't he? In fact he treats me like a precious vase or something. Like it matters.

The light is fading and the temperature is dropping. I need to keep going. Gareth starts to back out from the side of the bus shelter when he stops and listens. The sound of an engine, labouring slightly he thinks from coping with a gentle incline, is growing louder. He rolls forward and parks his wheelchair behind the shelter so he can see who is approaching from the valley without being observed from the road. In the same instant Gareth realises he has misjudged the distance, the Humvee from the castle goes past the shelter heading away down the hill.

It passes him so quickly, he doesn't have a chance to see who is driving but he can guess. The soldiers are looking for him and they are mobile. But in the Humvee which they found blown to pieces outside the castle when they arrived? Unless they have another one. But Gareth didn't see any sign of a second Humvee when he left the castle less than twenty minutes ago.

The dilemma facing Gareth now is what his next move should be. It was incredibly fortunate he happened to be out of sight behind the shelter at the moment they came past. He can hardly dive in a ditch if he meets them coming the other way. But if he doesn't get moving it will be very dark and very cold by the time he makes it to Aviemore, or any other of the local towns and villages.

Alternatively he could just give up and surrender as they will most likely be back within the hour. They will drive all the way to the main road and then start backtracking. But that's not an option is it? After what Gates has told them, it's obvious the sadistic bastard is just playing cat and mouse with us. There's no way a ruthless killer like him will hesitate with our fate once he's satisfied he has got all he can from us.

Michael seems to know a lot about the danger behind Gates's plan. There's no way he is just an activist. More like ex-military himself. Maybe he even worked on the development of HAARP. He might even know Gates from before. There is no doubt they are being lied to.

But what if this machine *is* some sort of God weapon which is going to destroy everything if they launch the earthquake attack against Iran? It looked as if Gates was ready to go. They are probably just waiting to capture me so they have plugged all the leaks. They will definitely kill us. There's no way Gates will risk there being anyone left to blow the whistle.

Gareth moves forward along the back of the bus shelter and out on to the road again. He points his wheelchair away from the castle and heads off.

Gates watches while two of his soldiers systematically lock Trent, Rachel, and Michael into wrist shanks in the interrogation room. Once they are securely locked down, Gates unhurriedly strolls round and checks the security of each set by yanking each of them hard by the chains they are attached to. Each set is bolted to the floor. He stares deeply into their eyes in turn, looking for their fears and weaknesses like the master torturer he is.

They all return his stare defiantly. Michael holds it the longest. Gates has his face an inch from Michael's.

"I'll derive the most satisfaction from breaking you Michael. Think you're indestructible don't you?" taunts Gates.

"You have no idea, Gates," replies Michael in a low, measured tone. "Have you used your machine to find the ark of the covenant yet?"

Gates studies Michael's face closely with what seems like something bordering on regret.

"You have missed your chance, Michael. Once again."

Trent snorts with derision.

"I don't have the first idea what you are talking about but even I understand that's a 'no you haven't'."

Gates turns to Trent and gestures to the metal pole above their heads which runs down the centre of the room. Open shackles dangle from a chain which is suspended over the pole.

"I would focus on what I'm going to do to your boy when my men round him up. He won't have got very far."

"Gareth is far more resourceful than you think," Trent says as defensively as he can.

"I'm sure he is. The proud father speaks. Let's see

how resourceful you all are when he is dangling like a pig in a slaughterhouse. And if he kills himself before my men find him, we will work our way through the others one by one until you agree to record my little video."

Gates runs a finger over his lips which are the colour of cooked liver.

Michael flexes the powerful muscles in his arms and yanks the chains angrily.

"That video will be a death warrant for Trent and you know that very well. The Iranians will use their secret service to hunt him down and kill Trent and his entire family and it will plunge two of the world's greatest powers into a war neither can possibly win."

"If everything goes to plan, that is correct." Gates nods.

"And then what?" asks Rachel.

"The people who really control the world have been working towards the final solution for two hundred years. The Brotherhood of the Red Shield has been in existence since the middle ages, since the Crusades, and the battle has been at full tilt ever since. Who do you think funded the Napoleonic wars, the outcome of the Battle of Trafalgar between the British and the French, who do you think funded the Nazis and the great United States of America after the Nazis were defeated? That wasn't supposed to be the outcome but always back a winner is our view," Gates says quietly.

"Are you claiming the same organisation has been behind every major event in two hundred years of history?" asks Trent disbelievingly.

"For the last two centuries at least, yes," nods Gates. "The development of HAARP was always going to be too much of a responsibility for individual governments. They can't understand the technology and have no stomach for the consequences of its use. It required organisations with more resolve and deeper pockets without Congress breathing down their necks at every turn."

"So you plan to start world war three and be there to take control when the radioactive dust settles?" Rachel says the words numbly, hardly daring to believe her own words.

"No, so far countries like Iran, North Korea and the Sudan have resisted our invitation to join our financial brotherhood. A major disaster will force Iran into seeing sense. We achieved the same thing using different means in Afghanistan, Iraq and Cuba before that. And a major disaster in Japan hid the real game plan—to halt their production of plutonium for Iran."

"Are you saying you murdered tens of thousands of innocent people in the Japanese tsunami to serve your political and financial ends?" gasps Rachel, incredulity thick in her voice.

"There's no such thing as innocence," scoffs Gates nastily. "If a people has enough resolve they will overthrow the wrongdoings of their leaders themselves as in Russia or the middle east."

"What about your wrongdoings?" laughs Michael cynically.

"They don't know who we are," Gates boasts. "We learned long ago that it is pointless seeking the approval of the masses. They are far too confused, lazy and stupid to be consulted. A benign dictatorship is the only solution."

"So you believe in dictatorship? That's not very evolved and aware is it?" asks Rachel.

"Action speaks louder than words you dim-witted

bitch," snaps Gates, his veneer of civility slipping. "Look at you. Fuck the first male who can get it up as soon as your husband's back is turned!"

Trent lunges forward furiously, snapping the chains tight. The cords in his neck are taut and his eyes bulge with anger.

"I should kill you right now, you fuck! Cut me loose and we'll settle this man to man!"

The two soldiers standing guard instinctively take a pace forward, raising their weapons and training them on Trent. Gates waves them away nonchalantly.

"I have no interest in wasting my breath on cowardly helicopter pilots."

"My husband is no coward!" yells Rachel angrily.

Gates drops his arm and turns to Rachel as if he has just noticed her for the first time—his usual trick to try to intimidate her.

"I don't think I'm incorrect. Your husband deserted his comrades and left them to the knives and sexual depravity of the Taliban while he ran away like a frightened dog."

A low growling echoes up the corridor leading to the interrogation room. A Satanic, evil growling full of menace and terror.

Gates turns to the open door.

"What the hell is that?"

The last orange rays of the setting sun sit in a crescent sliver on the mountains as Gareth trundles along the gravel road. He is saving the wheelchair's headlights as long as possible to conserve what battery power is left in the reserves. He knows if he switches them on they will give away his position to the returning soldiers anyway. The road is relatively straight with few corners so it's easy to stay on track.

Gareth is processing the information Gates told them about HAARP and what he plans to do with it. Does that go some way to explain the rash of earthquakes and tsunami around the world over the last few years? What was the word he used? Deniability? Yes, that was it. Deniability. The perfect weapon and the perfect battle. An unseen enemy using a weapon which is impossible to detect.

But what happens if it doesn't behave and backfires? Could that happen? What if it set off an earthquake down the massive fault he'd studied in school which runs right down the west coast of the US and into South America? They'd had a really big quake in Chile not so long ago hadn't they? And the weather? It seemed to be all over the place in the US and Europe, everywhere in fact.

Was it possible Gates was responsible? The weather bureaus and scientists seemed to be totally nonplussed at what was happening. If someone was triggering earthquakes and messing with the weather maybe that would explain it. All the funny noises people had been reporting at night. Dolphins and whales beaching themselves. Gareth had seen news reports on porpoises which had washed up looking like they had been scalded. Their hearing systems had exploded inside their heads.

No one had come up with a good explanation for thousands of blackbirds dropping out of the sky in Arkansas, or crabs which had washed up off the coast of England. 40,000 of them, the news had said. Apparently they had exploded as if they had decompressed suddenly. Then there were the millions of sardines off the coast of Chile which had washed ashore, coating the beaches for days.

Now he thought about it, his obsession with death had led him to hundreds of similar stories like that. Never mind the human death toll from the Indonesian tsunami, the big earthquake in Pakistan which followed shortly after it, then Haiti, Chile, China, Italy, and Japan with more to come no doubt. There had been killing on a really big scale of innocent people. Kids his age and younger. Much younger. What if Gates and his organisation were behind it all? Maybe it was population control?

Headlights approaching. The jumble of thoughts in Gareth's mind evaporate, leaving him scanning the road ahead for a possible hiding place. A sign to his right attracts his attention but he can't make out what it says. A road sign of some description. There must be a turning.

The Humvee is closing fast. Gareth judges it is still half a mile off. Hopefully the low light of dusk is cloaking his location enough to stop the soldiers picking him out in the throw from the bright headlights which sit two feet higher than a car, casting a pool of light further as a result.

Out of options, Gareth swings across the road and leaves the gravel road. As he passes the sign he catches a brief look at what it says—"Caution. Steps May Be Slippery When Wet."

He finds himself lurching down a flight of steep slate steps into the inky darkness. The wheels lurching around below him are similar in size to a scooter's and therefore can negotiate the lip of each step. Gareth rocks violently to and fro in a madcap seesaw motion, which threatens to unseat him at every sickening bounce. His five- point star harness keeps him wedged tightly in the seat but it will be all over if he interrupts his momentum by trying to brake or change direction away from straight down the steps.

The bright arc of the Humvee headlights passes by him above on the road. He dimly registers the sound of the engine decreasing as it gets further away. His crazily-rocking descent continues down another half-dozen steps and he suddenly sees the reason for them.

There is a natural pool fed by a waterfall directly in front of him. On any other occasion he might have even been struck by how beautiful it was, but the only thing on Gareth's mind is how to avoid running into it and drowning with the nearest assistance heading away from him steadily and his family helpless prisoners of that madman.

Gareth steers away from the course taking him into the inky black water. The last remnants of daylight pick out the slate pathway around the pool which is surrounded by a ring of stones. Somehow Gareth manages to bleed off enough speed and turn his wheelchair away from its certain end in the cold waters of the pool. He slows and then stops. His chest is heaving up and down from a mixture of adrenaline and exertion.

He waits for a few seconds while he gets his breath back and allows his eyes to adjust to the sudden darkness in the shadow of the track he has just left so unceremoniously.

🎵🎵🎵

The soldier's screaming escalates in pitch and volume rapidly by the sheer shock of his idea of reality leaving him so suddenly. The other soldier is jammed in behind him in the narrow space and can't see the reason for his terror. The screaming soldier tries to back as fast as he can out of the storage room while firing his weapon into the dark, but crashes into his compatriot. They tumble to the ground in a chaotic pile of arms, legs and weapons. The hollow metallic rattle of bullet casings striking the stone floor accompanies their screaming.

The soldier, still yelling in terror, fires another wild volley into the storage room before he suddenly reels back. Blood splashes everywhere.

The other soldier now sees the cause of his partner's terror and he too starts to scream in fear at the top of his lungs while he sprays bullets into the void. Blood covers him and he is beaten to the ground by an invisible force. Both of them recoil violently from an unseen hail of blows which rip and gouge them with astonishing ferocity. They are both dead before they hit the ground but the mauling continues. Invisible talons rip their flesh and there is a sickening crunch of bone as their bodies are mangled by their unseen assailant. Then it stops as suddenly as it started.

Silence falls. The ripped, mangled bloody bodies are a grisly sight. From some distance away in the darkness, the familiar sound of a harp picking out the same ghostly sequence of notes echoes along the walls of the underground complex.

The harp is audible in the interrogation room too where Trent, Rachel and Michael are chained to the floor. Gates's grip on his pistol tightens unconsciously.

"What the hell is that sound?" Gates repeats his question from earlier.

Michael looks up from where he is sitting on the metal chair bolted to the floor and gazes into Gates's eyes.

"It's the sound of death."

Gareth can see where the slate pathway leads away from the mysterious ring of stones sitting in silence around the bubbling waterfall which runs into the black pond. Cautiously he whirrs round the stones and switches his lights on. He has inwardly given up on the idea of escape and accepted his best plan is to try to get back to the castle and re-join Trent and Rachel.

His attempt to run has only highlighted how helpless he is on his own. Better to have strength in numbers until they find some sort of way out of this nightmare. Besides, Gates may have started to execute the others or torture them. Gareth tries to squeeze the thoughts out of his head as the resulting rising panic makes it impossible for him to think straight.

As he moves forward his headlights pick out a smooth path back onto the track. The road has bent round the waterfall and snaked back on itself, dropping 100 feet or so in the process. It explains why the Humvee surprised him. It would have been concealed until it crested the bend behind the waterfall. He is able to find the track easily. But he stops as he finds the gravel surface of his own personal road to Damascus.

The climb and bend are probably too difficult to negotiate in the wheelchair but if he sets off in the other direction towards Aviemore Gareth decides he will probably not make it far enough before losing power. Maybe he should just wait until someone comes along?

He starts to think of being collared by the soldiers as an option. Better than freezing to death out here. It is getting cold and he suffers from it more than most. Not being able to keep warm by moving is a massive disadvantage.

Gareth realises his rash attempt to escape wasn't the best thought through plan and he is beginning to seriously regret his actions. He could reverse into the shadows and wait for hypothermia to do its work. With the warmth of the sun gone, the temperature is dropping by the minute. The tips of his fingers and nose are starting to lose sensation. He saw a TV programme on the survival of crash victims once who were tipped into the sea from helicopters or boats into water and they lost consciousness in a scientific test within twenty minutes.

The programme had said water made you lose heat thirty times faster than air, but they hadn't taken having a stroke and not being able to move into consideration. Gareth thinks he might have a couple of hours at most before he will lose consciousness and fall into a sleep from which he will never recover.

As he remains motionless and undecided, a low growl is emitted somewhere out in the blackness. If Gareth was feeling the cold before, a chill goes to his bones which is primeval and deeply frightening. The thing has found him all the way out here and there is nothing he can do about it. The growling is closer and more insistent.

It is a long, deep lazy growl which reminds him of the beautiful big wild cats he loves to watch in nature programmes. Except he is now the prey. Two red dots appear directly in front of him, caught in the lights from his wheelchair which are still illuminated.

Transfixed, Gareth watches as they move closer to him and cross the road in front of him. Then they stop and he can feel eyes scrutinising him. He switches off his headlights but the floating red orbs continue to glow.

A vehicle is behind Gareth. He didn't hear it approach or stop but its headlights are throwing light across the road. Instinctively he wants to shout to switch off the lights, to try to hide. But it's a redundant instinct. Whatever that thing is, it can probably see him perfectly in pitch darkness, hear his heart beating and smell his fear. So the soldiers found him anyway. Maybe they can shoot it?

The malevolent red orbs blink once then they are gone. Here it comes, he thinks. It's going to rip me apart before the soldiers have time to even get out. Gareth hears the heavy diesel engine in the Humvee stop and doors open. Footsteps on gravel.

"What in God's name are you doing out here?" asks a voice. A voice with a Scottish accent.

Gareth is so surprised he forgets about the immediate threat from the beast and wheels round. He is dazzled by the headlights from the vehicle and can only see the vague outline of two figures who seem to glow in the glare of the Xenon headlights.

"I'm lost." Gareth says in his flat synthesised voice. "And cold."

"I'd say you were sonny," says the kindly local voice. "Let's get you in the back and we'll take it from there."

The long wheelbase Transit van idling in the darkness, not the Humvee after all, is equipped with a freight hoist and the two kindly men make light work of raising Gareth on the big metal plate until he is level with the large, empty space inside the van.

Gareth whirrs forward and they shut the big metal doors with a clang. The men make their way to the front of the van and jump in. The driver turns to Gareth from the high-backed three seat front of the van and looks at him approvingly.

"Good thing we've finished our deliveries for the day. We came up for a wee spot of lamping but found you instead," he laughs cheerily.

"What's lamping?" asks Gareth.

"That's a novel way to speak, Ben."

"My name's not Ben."

"It is as of five seconds ago. Ben as in Ben Hur."

The men laugh, not unkindly.

"My name's Gareth. I need to get up to the castle."

The driver extends a bottle of whisky towards Gareth between the seats.

"Nice to make your acquaintance Gareth. I'd offer you a wee dram of this fine single malt but neither of us can reach just now. I'm Gabriel and my friend here is Mickey."

"Thanks for rescuing me. I would have died if you hadn't come along."

"Oh I don't think so but it was fortuitous shall we say? You staying at the castle?"

"Yes. But would you mind dropping me before you reach the gate? And you should get away as quickly as possible when you do."

"As you like. Funny request but there we are. What were you doing down here anyway?"

"I was taking a stroll."

"You were?" Gabriel laughs again. "I have to admire your pluck young sir. May I suggest you take a friend next time?"

"I don't have any."

"Fair enough. Does that chariot of yours have a parking brake? We don't want you disappearing out the back on the way up there!"

"I'm fine thanks. Can we go?"

There is silence in the van as they drive up the hill. Gareth tries to get a better look at the two men in case they are yet more pieces in this twisted puzzle and are here to kill him and the others. They wouldn't be allies of Gates, he decides. They don't seem the military kind and have the air of genuinely gentle and peaceful types.

But then he got that impression from Michael at first. Gareth is still in two minds about that man. He might be schizophrenic, Gareth decides. He feels like your closest ally one minute and your enemy the next. Very confusing.

After barely more than 10 minutes of bouncing around in the back of the Transit, the headlights pick out the gate to the castle. I feel like I've been trapped by that castle for years, Gareth reflects to himself.

"This is you," Gabriel says.

They are the first words he's spoken since they set off. He does a u-turn on the gravel in one confident movement, despite the narrowness of the track and the 1,000 foot drop to one side of the gravel away down the face of the hill.

They lower Gareth to the ground outside the gate as requested. And then something very strange happens. No sooner has Gareth rolled off the metal plate of the hoist and turned the wheelchair round so he can look at the men to thank them, he is astonished to see the Transit van and the two men have disappeared into thin air.

Mystified, Gareth turns his wheelchair round to the right and left but there is nothing to suggest the van and the two men were ever there. Expecting to see tyre tracks where the van turned round, Gareth is nonplussed when he realises there is no trace.

Exhausted and cold, Gareth turns round again and heads up the long drive to the castle which looks more sinister than ever in the darkness.

# Crucifixion

Gates is studying Gareth's strained, tired features with a cruel fascination.

"What would possess you to try to escape, alone and in clothes more suited to a summer's day? You are either mad or stupid. Or perhaps you are both?"

Gates circles Gareth, his arms folded, as if he is studying a trapped butterfly in a bell jar.

Trent, a look of tortured misery on his face, Michael, dispassionate as ever, and Rachel, tears running down her face, remain chained to the concrete floor in the interrogation room. Gates turns his attention to the trio of helpless prisoners and smiles.

"Are you feeling that sense of helpless desperation yet? I sense two of you are possibly but your tall friend seems to lack the intelligence to realise you are all doomed."

Michael returns the mocking stare.

"Oh you mean me?"

"Yes, I mean you, the blonde giant. The Fallen Angel. The Watcher. The Nephilim," replies Gates mysteriously.

"And I am?" replies Michael laconically.

"You may feign indifference but I know what you are."

"Do you? How?"

"We have some of your contemporaries in our organisation. They are tall and blonde-haired like you. You are a race all of your own and when you've identified and understood what you and your type are, it's an easy task."

"Perhaps you are mistaken?"

"I don't think so. What I have learned is how...unsatisfying it is to use persuasion with you people," Gates says, seemingly amused.

But then he spins round and grabs Gareth by the front of his v-neck jumper and pulls him up cruelly tightly against his five point racing harness.

"However the mute will be a lot more fun."

It's too much for Trent, who tries to lunge forward. Once again he is easily restrained by the thick chains. They rattle noisily as he twists and turns wildly. Gates wags a finger in admonishment at Trent.

"Now, now, chopper boy. That won't do any good at all."

Gates barks orders at the two remaining soldiers who are standing at ease by the interrogation room door. Trent's face is distorted by fury and mounting horror as the full intent of what Gates is planning to do fully registers with him.

"No!" is all Rachel can screams before she breaks down and starts sobbing.

Michael leans back in the metal chair bolted to the floor and a look of untroubled amusement slowly spreads across his face. A look which does not go unnoticed by Gates.

"Now this is interesting," he observes. "The Nephilim, the Fallen Angel, is not bothered by the prospect of violence against a completely innocent and helpless young man. Unlike his parents. Are all Nephilim sociopaths like you?"

Michael shrugs noncommittally.

"Are you asking if I experience empathy? You're the expert. You tell me."

The soldiers push Gareth under the chain suspended over the pole in the centre of the interrogation room. They attach Gareth face first to a wooden stave with chains secured with climbing caribiners and cut his jumper and shirt away with knives until his upper half is naked and exposed.

They start to winch him out of the chair with a pulley. He dangles helplessly in the air as if he is being crucified. The harsh lights cast the shadow of a slowly-spinning crucifix across the floor as Gareth rotates.

"I hope the irony of using your own caribiners to winch your son up in preparation for our little ritual is not lost on you Trent. I thought it was a nice touch," gloats Gates as he twirls a long whip into a bucket of water. He sees Trent staring in horror at the cruel-looking instrument.

"The water is salted. It makes the sting of the whip so much worse." Gates stops twirling the whip as if a thought has just occurred to him. "I take it his paralysis does not prevent him from feeling sensation? All this theatre will be for nought otherwise."

"He can feel everything just like anyone else you sadist!" screams Rachel. "Why don't you leave the poor boy alone? Take it out on me. I deserve it a whole more than that poor innocent boy."

Gareth slowly rotates helplessly as the chains elevate him free of the chair. He stops spinning as they straighten out and he locks eyes with his father. His eyes are silently pleading. Trent turns his gaze slowly to look at Gates who is enjoying every second.

"OK that's enough. I'll do it. I'll record the video

and you can do your worst with it," Trent almost mumbles incoherently. His body is trembling with rage and fear.

"Louder please. I may have misheard. I thought you said you would record the video," retorts Gates.

Trent tries to pull himself together. "That's right. I'll do it," he says in a ragged broken rasp.

Gates cocks one ear theatrically.

"Louder!"

"I'll do it!" Trent manages to half shout, half croak his statement.

"Louder!" insists Gates.

"Why don't you shut the fuck up and just do it?" asks Michael evenly.

Gates turns to Michael and dangles the tip of the whip less than an inch in front of his face.

"Oh you are the interesting one. So good at reading people."

Trent's bloodshot eyes widen and he croaks "No-o-o-o-!" as the whip blurs through the air and lashes Gareth in a diagonal on his back. Gareth doesn't react whatsoever—he is incapable—but he screws his eyes shut.

Against the rising cacophony of Trent and Rachel begging, imploring, cursing Gates to stop, the whip flashes through the air and strikes Gareth across his body again and again.

His eyes gleaming with sadistic pleasure, Gates says to Michael, "You might recognise this. Book of Enoch, Chapter 61 from the Ethiopic translation if memory serves me right..."

Gates draws back the whip. *"Then shall the kings..."*
He lands the blow.
*"The princes, and all who possess the earth, glorify Him who*

*has dominion over all things."*

The whip hisses through the air and lands another stinging impact. A thin arc of blood sprays across the floor.

*"Him who was concealed for from eternity the Son of Man was concealed."*

Another blow. Tears stream from Gareth's tightly-shut eyes as tiny cubes of his flesh flick though the air .

*"Whom the Most High preserved in the presence of His power and revealed to the elect."*

Gates finally stops and wipes away the sweat running into his eyes. A lattice of red weals has been drawn on Gareth's back and his blood runs in a wet curtain down his torso until it soaks into his trousers then drips from his legs onto the floor.

Gareth is crying silently. His impassive face is a bizarre contrast to the agonising pain he is feeling. Mercifully, he passes out on the impromptu wooden cross at that moment and his tightly screwed up eyes relax. Blood continues to drip from the angry weals onto the concrete floor three feet below in a messy circle as he spins slowly in mid air.

Gates drops the whip into the bucket with contempt. Trent is sobbing uncontrollably. Snot bubbles out of his nose and runs down his face. Rachel has passed beyond hysteria and is frozen like a statue. Michael is leaning back in his metal chair, his face is impassive and his eyes are closed as if he is sleeping.

Then a single tear clearly escapes from his left eye and runs down his handsome face. He doesn't try to wipe it away.

♆♆♆

Gareth is floating down a beautiful river in the bottom of a wooden dugout boat. The sun is warm on his face and there is no trace of the beating he has just endured. His eyes are closed and he seems to be sleeping. There is a distant sound of what sounds like babies crying coming from the river bank.

Gareth dangles one hand in the warm water. The bright sunlight spangles off the disturbed water around his fingers as they trail through the tiny eddies. Annoyingly, the crying is growing louder and disturbing the perfect tranquillity of his reverie. He sits up and runs a hand through his hair, which has somehow managed to grow down to his shoulders. He has also developed a neat beard and moustache. His hand lingers on his face in surprise as he runs his fingers through the unfamiliar hair on his face.

The fact he is moving freely is not lost on Gareth. But it's as if he has always been able to move. He raises his hand and looks at it with a mixture of astonishment and pride. He rotates it slowly, savouring the motor control of the tendons and muscles which are delicately moving it.

He shields his eyes from the glare of the sun and looks for the source of the crying. As it gets louder or he slips closer, he's not sure which it is, Gareth can make out some women dressed head to toe in dark brown and white garbs. Their heads are covered in white and they extend the material to conceal their faces. They protectively clutch white bundles to their chests as they hurry along the riverbank toward him.

They arrive at some thick patches of reeds and hurriedly place the bundles amongst the long stalks which are topped with the distinctive brown furry cylinders. The reeds wave and sway gently in the breeze. The bundles must be babies as the noise is reaching a crescendo of wailing. The agitated women are crying too and the collective noise sounds pretty awful to Gareth.

A group of what look like soldiers in leather breast-plates and helmets are approaching from the distance behind the women with an air of dark purpose. The women see the soldiers and scatter in different directions. The soldiers draw their stubby little swords and daggers. They break into a run along the riverbank, spreading out as they do.

One by one they catch the women and plunge their weapons into their bodies. The women don't fight back but seem to accept their fate with resignation. They don't even cry out. In diverting the attention of the soldiers they have successfully led them away from the crying babies amongst the reeds.

Gareth slides into the bottom of the boat and peeks over the top to see if the babies have escaped the same fate as their mothers. But one soldier has heard the crying and he calls to the others to join him. They wade up to their waists amongst the reeds and stab their swords down repeatedly until all the crying has stopped. Gareth starts to sob in horror at what he has just witnessed.

There is a soft knock from the end of the dugout. Gareth has passed the murderous soldiers and is some distance downstream from them. He looks up to see what has caused the noise. There is a little boat made from reeds with a makeshift tent on the top. It's made from the same material as the dresses the women were wearing.

Gareth fishes the makeshift raft out of the water and dumps it into the bottom of the boat. He can hear crying from the little tent. Gingerly, he opens the flaps at the end and looks inside. Gareth's own face meets him. He is crying with the sound of a baby. Gareth lurches back in shock and hits his head on the edge of the dugout. He slumps back, unconscious from the blow.

When Gareth regains his senses, the first thing he notices is the incredible heat. He tries to sit up but can't. His hands are restrained and they hurt really badly. Really, really badly. So do his feet. He tries to look down but the movement of his head is restricted to. There is a rope tied around his neck and his head is pressed against a rough surface which feels and smells like wood.

The hot sun is making the rich, sticky sap adhere to the back of his neck. Some of it runs into his half-closed eyes and makes them sting. The rivulet of sap pools into his eye socket and then spills over down his face and into his mouth.

Gareth licks his lips to taste the sap. But it's not sap, it's blood. His blood. He cranes his neck sideways and he can just see out of the corner of his eye that a crude metal spike has been driven through the palm of his hand. Dried blood is caked around his wrist which is bound to the wooden plank with rope. The rope has turned black from his blood.

He tries to move his feet which point down and overlap but he can't shift them as they too are pinned in position by another metal spike. When he looks ahead he can see the sky so he must be lying on the ground.

His mouth is dry and as he runs his tongue over his lips he can feel how cracked they are. He is so thirsty. His back is burning from heat or something. He tries to wriggle around but can hardly move as he is so restricted by the rope and the horrible metal spikes. His whole body hurts with a symphony of pain. Is this how he dies finally? What is he doing here? How did this happen?

He can feel the unrelenting rays of the sun burning his groin. He must be completely naked. He can feel hot swirls of air dancing across his entire body. To his horror and revulsion, he can feel the blood entering his penis. It starts to swell and stiffen. What if someone sees him? He is helpless. The pain wracking his body only makes his arousal worse. Soon his naked penis is erect and throbbing. Little tongues of air tease and tickle him.

"Water."

He croaks the word through his dry, swollen lips. His tongue feels too large for his mouth and it is so dry it sticks to the roof of his mouth. Someone is close by. He feels their shadow cross the hot sun, bringing him a little respite from the searing heat. A cooling twist of wet material is pressed gently on his dessicated lips and drops of water trickle into his mouth. It is the most gorgeous feeling he has ever experienced. A woman's soft lips caress his cheek and more water is squeezed into his mouth.

He is about to express his thanks when he feels a hand on his erect member. There is a gentle rhythmic movement up and down his aching penis. As he feels the light, gentle motion of the unseen hand, the moist lips cover his and kiss him. The soft warmth is delicious. He almost forgets about the agonising pain from the metal spikes hammered through his hands and feet.

The movement up and down his penis slowly increases in intensity and the lips move across his face to kiss his eyes, nose and ears. They return to his mouth and a moist tongue slips into his refreshed mouth and twists around his tongue.

The hand sliding up and down his penis grips him

more firmly as whoever is touching him senses he is about to come. When he does the release is immense and he cries out in ecstasy as the mouth on his bites his lower lip until he tastes more blood.

And then she is gone. He is alone again. He strains his head round to see who she is but there is no one there. He winces as he realises he has something sharp around his head. It is the reason for the blood which ran into his eye.

Gareth sighs a long exhalation of pain and sadness, ejecting a mouthful of blood and spittle at the same time. He coughs and starts to choke. The wooden cross he is cruelly pinned to suddenly lurches and starts to move.

He is slowly raised into a vertical position. The effect of gravity on the metal spikes driven into his hands and feet is agonising. The ropes have contracted as a result of being soaked, he assumes, in his blood. Mercifully tight, they take a little of the weight and lessen what would be unbearable pain otherwise.

Now completely vertical, Gareth can just about make out a white walled city below him. He is on a hill overlooking the parched valley. The bright sun makes him squint and it is hard to see anything. Gareth keeps very still, whimpering slightly to himself more out of desperation than pain.

He can hear voices and laughing. A cruel stabbing sensation in his torso distracts him from his other wounds. Someone has thrust a vicious point into his side. He feels the metal slice his insides then grind around agonisingly before being withdrawn. Fresh blood pours down his side and drips off his toes.

A deep, Satanic growls reverberates around his head. So Abaddon—wasn't that what they called the beast of the pit—has chosen this moment in some sort of parallel reality to claim him. Was this what this all about? He has been forsaken by every last person before he descends into hell. Is this to be his punishment for what he did to his mother and his twin brother?

"I'm sorry," he cries out in a tortured sob.

"Please forgive me!"

He feels large, razor claws sinking into his neck and chest.

Gareth gasps in pain and lurches forward from the cross into the arms of Rachel.

He is lying on the hard concrete surface of the interrogation room with Rachel and Trent crouched over him. They share a look of pure horror.

Gareth is back in his frozen body once again. His back is burning with incredible pain. Rachel has a bunched-up piece of bloody material pressed against his forehead.

"Oh Gareth we thought we'd lost you."

She trickles some water into his mouth, forgetting he has no swallowing reflex and he starts to choke. Trent takes hold of his shoulders and raises him so his head is vertical. The pain is excruciating from his back.

His father clears his mouth and airway with a finger then gives him CPR by blowing into his mouth while clasping his nostrils shut. Gareth starts to breathe normally almost straight away.

The three of them huddle together on the cold floor while Rachel and Trent sob with the quiet desperation of defeat. Unnoticed by his sobbing parents, Gareth blinks and when his eyes open, they have become feline tawny yellow vertical slits. He blinks again and his eyes return to normal.

The interrogation room door opens. Gates and his two remaining faithful soldiers enter. Gates looks at the pathetic huddle on the cold floor with contempt. His eyes settle on Michael. He points at him.

"Release tallboy but keep him cuffed. We can't trust him."

The soldiers unlock the heavy clasps as they simultaneously click handcuffs onto Michael's wrists.

Michael gestures for them to keep their distance.

"Please don't touch me. You're not worthy."

The uglier soldier shrugs.

"Fine with me Herr Michael. Move it."

He prods Michael with the barrel of his M17 Herstal.

"Please come with us Michael. Oh, and bring the boy. He requires some urgent attention," orders Gates.

"If you are planning to harm my son further, I will kill you more slowly than I originally planned," snarls Trent who looks anything but capable of doing anyone harm currently.

Gates waves away the threat with a dismissive shrug. Michael gently scoops Gareth's bleeding and broken body into his arms and follows Gates. The second soldier pushes Gareth's wheelchair behind them, with his gun resting across the arms.

The door closes behind them. Trent and Rachel are alone for the first time since the revelation about her involvement with Michael.

Trent looks at his wife for a long time and says in a resigned, weary voice, "Are you ready to talk now?"

# Meltdown

In a field behind the castle, a curious array of what resemble radio aerials stand in near silence. The low humming sound of the powerful electrical current powering the HAARP array is the only imperfection.

Numbering one hundred and eighty in total, laid out neatly in twelve by fifteen rows, the thirty foot high metal stanchions each have a complex array of wire around their crown like halos. The metal poles are connected with taut wires.

The 3,600,000 watt energy generated by the pylons beams upwards thirty miles to the ionosphere above their target, Iran. Sitting between the Arabian and Eurasian tectonic plates which form part of the slowly-moving sections of the earth's crust, Iran is a natural candidate for severe earthquakes.

A new event, as the scientists call it, will not come as a surprise as quakes in the region are common. A really big one, an 8.0 or 9.0 magnitude quake on the Richter scale, would be in the top one percent globally. A quake on that scale is a killer. The ground seems to become liquid, whole towns are flattened in less than a minute, thousands are killed, trapped in the rubble of collapsing buildings.

Until you have experienced what seems like the whole world shaking and rocking, where there is nowhere to run, when everything around you falls down, huge clouds of concrete dust obscure everything and rise like an atomic bomb, you cannot begin to imagine the terror and chaos.

The kind of chaos the Devil himself rejoices in. Terror, fear and suffering feed the Devil's power and control. Elements which manifest everywhere in the modern disintegrating world.

The sheer level of casualties in a major earthquake could be thought of as Satanic in their magnitude. Thousands will die in a quake immediately, thousands more will perish as they lie buried by tons of rubble. Occasionally someone is rescued two weeks after a quake. More often than not they are pulling bodies, instead of the living, from the pancaked buildings.

The cries generally stop after 24 hours.

And unlike an atomic bomb, similar to those the US dropped on Japan at the end of the Second World War, or on a much smaller scale, a terrorist car bomb, the attack, if it is an attack, is totally deniable and undetectable.

How can you find something unless you know what you're looking for in the first place? There's no need for deniability if there isn't even an accusation to rebuff in the first place.

To fully comprehend what Gates and his organisation intend to achieve, it is necessary to know something about the way the natural earth works.

To accomplish Gates's plan the energy from the Bothy Castle array is being mirrored from identical facilities in Gakona, southern Alaska, Costa Rica, the Falkland Islands, Norway and Menwith Hills in England.

All five facilities are bombarding the high atmosphere with a total energy concentration of 15,000,000 watts. The thin air of the ionosphere is bulging as a result of the unnatural heating of an area which is normally minus fifty degrees Celsius.

How this creates an earthquake is very odd. The concentrated beams produce a meteorologically artificial area of super-low pressure similar to a hurricane. The air pressure at sea level drops to an unprecedented low level. It releases the pressure on the sea bed of billions of tons of water above an already unstable fault line where two tectonic plates are grinding against each other with incalculable pressure.

A sudden shift in pressure on the one thousand mile long crack in the rock between the plates releases the lock keeping the two separate bands of rock stable. The sudden subduction, or movement of the plates, generates a seismic shock of two separate wavelengths of destruction which rocket through the surrounding rock at the speed of sound.

The shorter wavelength will arrive first and shake the ground but as the second, longer shockwave arrives it will build pressure and shockwave after shockwave will crash into the back of the one in front. The ground shakes to and fro, sometimes for minutes at a time.

If the city you live in is built on a soft sedimentary rock, like limestone, and surrounded by granite, as in the case of Port Au Prince in Haiti, which grew and prospered on the limestone flood plain of an estuary like with so many seaports, it will only require a relatively small shock to bring a city crashing down.

The last naturally-caused earthquake to flatten Haiti is a relatively small 7.1 magnitude. The shock waves race through the granite surrounding Port Au Prince easily without slowing down much, due to its crystalline composition which offers little resistance to shock waves. The limestone in the centre of the city slows the racing shock waves down and they crash into each other, causing a bottleneck of energy which amplifies the effect many times over.

Flimsy, badly built, top heavy concrete structures shake to and fro then collapse, burying thousands of people under the rubble.

More than 100,000 people die.

Tsunamis, which are caused by such earthquakes under the ocean, become bigger and more destructive for surprisingly similar reasons, although their magnitude is quickly amplified by the relative steepness of the incline of the sea floor of coastal waters.

The steeper the shelf near the seashore as the tsunami approaches, the higher the wave.

To Gates and his compatriots, Iran's coastline presents a near perfect disaster profile for combined earthquake and tsunami damage.

The double whammy of the HAARP weapon they have invented is that it runs at an extremely low frequency, 2.5 gigahertz, exactly the same frequency which triggers earthquakes.

This phenomenon is first discovered by a Serbian genius called Nikola Tesla in the US in the 1920s. Tesla makes headlines by triggering local earthquakes repeatedly when he starts conducting tests.

As the concerted bombardment builds towards triggering a new, gigantic quake along Iran's coastline, strange things start happening around the world which have a bizarrely familiar pattern to them.

Millions of fish die off the coastline of Chile and float to the surface in a silvery shroud covering tens of miles.

Crabs which appear to have been cooked from the

inside are washed ashore off Dungeness on the south coast of Britain.

There are news reports of mysterious sightings of porpoises off the coast of Oregon floating dead in the water which have the appearance of being burned. Their natural sonar system of their inner ear is damaged beyond belief.

Millions of blackbirds fall from the sky in Arkansas. They die inexplicably at the exact same moment.

There is one piece of information the news channels, local fishermen, scientists and coast guards who witness the sudden rash of anomalies are missing.

The deaths coincide exactly with more HAARP arrays being switched on in the same locations as before which caused exactly the same pattern of animal deaths. The arrays are powered up in a carefully planned ignition sequence, masterminded by one maverick US Army officer.

General Seth Japheth Gates.

Originally commander of the "Screaming Eagles" 101st Airborne Division based in Fairbanks, Alaska, it was just a short hop to Gakona, south east Alaska, where he was seconded to the first HAARP facility to be built in the tiny hamlet of Gakona, population 218.

Gates immediately saw the potential to weaponise a device which was capable of so many undetectable activities. It wasn't location critical and could transmit a computer-controlled radio beam to anywhere around the globe from the same base by using the ionosphere as a mirror to effectively bounce a radio beam off and negate the blocking effect of the curvature of the earth.

What his masters at the Defense Department in Washington didn't know when they put gates in charge of the new system in Gakona after his very successful tenure at Camp X-Ray, Guantanamo Bay in Cuba in 2002, was his much deeper alliance to the Brotherhood, a worldwide group of such secrecy and power that no one in Gates's life has the first idea of his allegiance.

Which makes Gates a very dangerous man.

Martin Cusack, ex-Alaskan Iditarod dogsled winner, is standing amongst his large fifty-strong pack of Huskies on his property just south of Wasilla, Alaska. The sudden frantic barking from the dogs has woken him from a fitful sleep. It is light almost twenty hours a day in Alaska at this time of year and he never sleeps that well anyway.

The dogs buck their light chains secured to small concrete blocks by their individual doghouses. The racket is deafening. To anyone unused to fifty excited dogs barking crazily at the same time, the noise would make it impossible to think straight. But to Martin, it's normal.

He's made of pretty solid stuff, which he proved when he cut the top of his thumb off just before the start of the Iditarod a few years back chainsawing spruces for firewood. He ran the entire 1400 mile race across the frozen miles of Alaska minus a section of thumb on the same hand he used to operate the sled brake and care for his sled team of twelve dogs.

Born in Switzerland, Martin was already used to the cold before he settled in Alaska so windchill of minus thirty or forty degrees Celsius was not new. Not that he'd experienced those sort of temperatures for a few years now. The problem these days was not having enough snow at times. Alaska, famous for its frozen wastes, was short on snow for a lot of the winter.

And the familiar strange, spiralling blue cone in the sky above his head accompanied by a very low frequency droning sound is doing nothing to improve his confidence for conditions in the coming February, traditionally the coldest month of the year, for the next Iditarod. Similar anomalies like the thing above him right now had been appearing for the last five years from time. He'd grown tired of reporting them because no one ever believed him.

The official explanation was a variation of the Northern Lights, the Aurora Borealis, which Martin, and everyone in Alaska north of Fairbanks, was used to seeing. But even that was becoming a common sight over the far south of Alaska where Martin lived.

Folks as far south as Juneau in Alaska and across east in North and South Dakota, Wyoming and Montana were seeing it on occasion these days too. That was because magnetic north was creeping east and down to the south he'd been told. Four hundred miles in ten years they reckoned.

But this is something different. It just isn't natural and the dogs seem to agree. They are responding to the sound more than the weird lights twisting and turning in a blue and green ribbed cone which stretch all the way across the light night sky to the east.

They are beautiful, true enough, but Martin is convinced these weird lights which had appeared irregularly then more frequently over the last few years are connected somehow to the warmer winters and lack of snow around him.

Much further south in the US, whole states are being paralysed by freezing weather because of a shift in the Jetstream while Martin is standing in his thermals looking at the weird sight in the sky. Chicago and the

Great Lakes have been a deep freeze for two months this winter. Illinois is a chilly winter state but not like that. Houses facing the lakes have been flooded then frozen when the waters glaze over. When the winds get up, the ice is pushed onto the land like a glacier. It grinds the houses all along the shore of the Great Lakes into matchwood.

Martin heads into the house to get his VCR to capture some footage of the strange lights. When he is inside rooting around for the battered old camera, the dogs suddenly fall silent. The low hum has stopped. Martin steps outside and looks up. The lights have gone and the long dusk of the Alaskan sky is empty once again.

♆♆♆

"Dammit," mutters Gates under his breath.

He is bent over the long, curved control console bathed in eerie blue light. Alarms are sounding from multiple points. Michael stands behind him. The desk matches his size perfectly. Gates is dwarfed by the scale of the room.

One soldier has been left in the ER to dress Gareth's wounds, the second stands guard over Michael who is still in handcuffs.

"So has your train set blown up?" he asks to Gates's back.

"It seems we have exceeded the power supply available globally. That or the magnetosphere is draining the electromagnetic field faster than we can charge it," Gates replies almost absent-mindedly. He is focussed on the readouts from the myriad instruments.

"Maybe I can help?" offers Michael.

Gates twists his head round sharply in irritation.

"You? Don't be ridiculous. You don't know the first thing about this system. I have a Masters in just about every discipline and I helped build this room and all the systems around the castle," says Gates.

"But you don't know how to produce more power do you?" asks Michael bluntly.

"I'll figure it out. I always do. There will be a solution," Gates replies, his voice thick with tension.

Michael walks round to face Gates, blocking his view of the console and the slowly-increasing sea of red warning lights.

"I can give you the Ark."

"The what?" asks Gates blankly.

"The Ark. Of The Covenant. The original HAARP device which the children of Israel used to destroy the Philistine stronghold of Jericho with the same principle as your machine. The device Moses used to part the Red Sea and the same technology the Egyptians utilised to lift thousand-ton blocks into place to build the pyramids."

"How?"

"It's accessible right here in the castle. But there is a problem." Michael says softly.

"Which is?" replies Gates impatiently.

"It is hidden in a parallel dimension guarded by Abaddon, the angel demon of the pit, the jailer of the Devil himself. If the Ark comes here, so might he and he isn't very nice."

Gates turns back to the console.

"OK you've lost me there. Stop wasting my time and get out of my way."

Michael is unswayed. "I can prove it to you."

"How long have we known each other?" Trent asks Rachel. He sounds and looks like he is ready to give up. She glances at him and feels the divide which has grown between them.

"Too long to let this destroy us. Trent, if you don't believe me, fine, but I'm sorry for what I've done."

"Was Gareth right? How many more?"

Rachel looks crestfallen and she gives slightly as the guilt washes over her.

"One other. A long time ago."

Trent winces visibly and his features settle into a look of dull pain.

"Do you have any idea how that makes me feel? To think I wasn't good enough. That you were going from the arms of some other man to mine and fooling me? How can we ever come back from that? Fucking that blonde giant right under my nose in the middle of a nightmare. How can I ever trust you again? Twice? It *will* happen again won't it?"

Rachel studies Trent's face for a long time, searching for the right words.

"Trent...darling. I started to feel more like your carer than your wife and you let that happen. I have worked so hard to make things, you, right. But there is only so much one person can do. Do you ever consider what it's like for me, supporting your mood swings and depression? And Gareth. He was a normal, happy little boy when I first met him. Before the stroke. Before Delissa was—died."

Trent rubs his face. He has never felt so tired in his life.

"When you think about it objectively I suppose, I was an illicit affair too. You slept with me long before Delissa died." He states matter of factly.

"Oh come on Trent. You were there too. I loved—love—you. And Gareth. There's the most incredible young man inside that prison of a body of his. I know that. We both remember what a great kid he was don't we? But I'm just not in love with you anymore. I love you but there is something missing. I'm sorry but there it is."

"I want to change that. I think I do anyway. But infidelity is a habit. You'll do it again."

"I won't if I you can give me what I need Trent."

"And that is?"

There is silence between them as Rachel searches for an answer.

"That's the problem. I don't know."

"Oh great. That's a real help. Take Michael. What does he have I don't?"

"I wanted to try and explain that but I can't. And even I could, I don't think as a man you'd want to hear grisly details."

"What does that mean?"

"It seems to me that men want to know what the opposition have that they think they don't. Although they do of course. But it's an impossible question to answer for a woman."

"Try me. It can't get any worse."

"He's like an animal."

"And that's a good thing?"

"He's dangerous. You know that. And powerful. I'm not even sure he's human. It was like he manipulated me against my will."

"So now you're telling he hypnotised you against your will also?"

"Yes. But if you really want to know, it was incredible. I have never experienced anything like it. Yet his...thing was cold like it was dead."

"You know what? You're right. Men can't handle the details. But here's one detail for you."

Rachel looks up. Her hands lay passively in her lap.

"Here it comes," she thinks to herself.

"If we ever get out of this nightmare, I think I want a divorce Rachel."

Gates and Michael are standing by the open elevator. Gates and the soldier lean forward until their heads disappear inside the open dark square of the safety cage. Gates's head reappears.

"What are we looking for exactly?" he asks Michael sceptically.

His pistol is aimed at Michael's sternum. Michael raises his handcuffed wrists in a sort of supplication.

Gates shakes his head and gestures impatiently with the gun.

"If I release you, the first thing you are going to do is try to kill me."

"That's the gamble. Your plan to destroy Iran versus your distrust of me. Which is it to be?" Michael shrugs.

He knows he is holding all the aces.

Gates digs the soldier, who still has his head in the elevator, in the ribs with his Beretta.

"Uncuff him. But watch him. If he does anything to threaten me, kill him."

The soldier nods, leans his rifle against the elevator and removes the cuffs. Michael rubs his sore wrists then steps forwards. Gates and the soldier both point their guns at him. Michael waves them away.

"Not cool. Please stand back and let me work. The

portal to the ark lies at the bottom of the lift shaft. It has been there since the wizard of the Knights Templar hid it in 1295 to protect it from falling into the hands of the Roman Catholic church before they were rounded up and put to death by 1310. But to do so, the wizard Merlin had to invoke the most powerful and deadly angel he could, Abaddon. He was such a powerful demon he even kept Lucifer, Satan himself, prisoner for a millennium. Legend has it he kept the Devil amused by playing Archangel Gabriel's harp to him."

Gates dismisses Michael's words with a distaste bordering on disgust.

"Enough lunatic ranting. Do something to make me believe you or I'll shoot you where you stand."

Without another word, Michael turns and bows before the elevator door, pressing his hands together as if in prayer as he does so. He bows his head, closes his eyes and breathes in and out slowly. Over his deep and rhythmic breathing he begins to intone what sounds to Gates like a spell or curse in a language of which he has no knowledge. Maybe something ancient like Hebrew or Aramaic, he guesses.

Michael's strange articulation is interspersed with clicks and guttural sounds almost as if he is speaking English but backwards. Michael's brow is furrowed in concentration and he longer seems to be aware of his surroundings. His hands fluctuate from prayer position to clenching into tight balls.

As his voice rises in pitch and intensity, he gestures forward with his hands into the dark space of the elevator. Almost imperceptibly, the lights in the corridor brighten and the background low hum of electrical power grows louder.

Suddenly Michael stops chanting in the strange language and steps back. As he does so he grabs the soldier with one hand and pushes him into the elevator. A protest is half-formed in the soldier's throat but it is cut off as he disappears into the gloom. There is silence. Stunned, Gates shoves the barrel of the gun in Michael's back.

"What the hell did you just do?"

He leans forward nervously and peers into the elevator. Then he steps back. The soldier has disappeared.

"Get that soldier back here. Right now! Or I'll shoot," snarls Gates.

"I'm afraid that's not possible. Abaddon requires a sacrifice. It's part of the contract."

"Do I have the power I need?" asks Gates, releasing the pressure of his gun which is still jammed into Michael's back.

"Yes. But I am going to say this only once Gates."

"Say what?"

"You need to treat me with much more respect."

"Why?"

"Because you have no idea who or what you are dealing with."

Trent is facing a camera in the video control room. He blinks slowly and licks his dry lips nervously. Gates is squinting through the viewfinder of the professional broadcast camera. He fiddles with the settings and glances at a TV monitor balanced on the fader desk. Trent's image blurs in and out of focus and then settles down. The brightness shifts around until that too is acceptable to Gates. His Beretta sits on top of the monitor.

"What do you want me to say Gates?" asks Trent

wearily.

"You see the big glass on the camera? In just two shakes that will have exactly what I want you to say on it. It will scroll up as you read. Don't chase the words. I will be controlling the speed of the roller so just read at a nice, natural pace. Sit up straight and keep your eyes on what you're reading. If you keep glancing round it will make you appear shifty. Think of Presidential Speeches and you'll be fine."

Trent snorts in disgust and shakes his head slowly.

"Thanks for the media training. Shame it will be wasted. I'm incriminating myself and signing my own death warrant into the bargain. And for my whole family. How am I supposed to look Presidential? I'll be the most wanted man on the planet."

Gates appears quite cheerful. He's enjoying this.

"Good isn't it? This won't be the first—or last—occasion we will have launched an attack like this but it will be the first time I've had someone claim responsibility. The political fallout should be interesting."

"It's not a campaign for chrissakes Gates. It's murder. Thousands, hundreds of thousands of people will die."

"As I thought I'd already explained there's no such thing. The blood of a nation is on the hands of the people. It's all about denial. For example, Iran is training young woman in their thousands right now to become assassins. That's not a country practising democracy and freedom."

"And I suppose the recruits joining Homeland Security's 350,000 force are somehow different?

"Of course. They are there to protect freedom and democracy."

"As long as everyone does what they're told? Is that

what you'd call fluid democracy? Democracy as long as you're in charge?"

Gates waves away the argument dismissively.

"Everything is ready. When that red light on top of the glass goes on, it means we are recording and you start speaking. And sound like you mean it. If you don't I'll simply shoot you and you know I don't make empty threats."

"I see now where your enemies learned their craft while they were at Camp X-Ray."

The red light blinks on and Gates cues Trent with a finger as if he is a chat show host.

Trent pauses momentarily, weighing up a bullet against continuing to participate in this nightmare. He keeps his eyes fixed on the glass with the round, black lens of the camera lurking behind it. He thinks of the computer HAL in '2001 A Space Odyssey'. Another heartless monster constructed from chips and wires.

Technology was always going to be the thing which killed us he thinks ruefully.

Trent starts to read.

Martin Cusack is sleeping under a huge bearskin. His wife slumbers peacefully next to him. The familiar humming is back. It restarts and almost immediately, Martin's eyes half-open and he looks around the familiar surroundings. The Huskies chained up outside in the dog-pen start to bark in ones and twos until they are all barking lustily.

He groans and pulls a pillow over his head.

# The Final Solution

Not really a wave, more of a bulge in the ocean, a mass of water swells in the ocean off the coast of Iran. Seconds ago, 1200 kilometres of seabed heaved upwards forty metres displacing trillions of kilograms of seawater. It's as if a giant rug has been tugged and tossed in the air by unseen hands.

The shock wave created by the vast amount of water suddenly displaced races towards the coastline at near the speed of sound. As the head of the shockwave rockets through the two kilometre-deep water, fishing boats, buoys and seabirds resting on the surface bob up and down a metre and a half. It's almost completely undiscernible from a regular wave.

It triggers an alarm on the GOES 13 satellite 300 kilometres above the relatively thin veneer of the earth's atmosphere. Hoisted into space by a Delta IV rocket from Space Launch Complex 37B at Cape Canaveral Air Force Station in Florida on May 24, 2006, the satellite is fitted with synthetic aperture radar developed by a technology company which is capable of measuring even tiny millimetric changes in the mass of the oceans.

The scientists controlling it at the National Environmental Satellite, Data, and Information Service, NESDIS for short, are alerted to the two metre high moving bulge. It is now ninety seconds since the tectonic plates running down the coast of Iran on the Eurasian Plate suddenly moved the Arabian Plate forty metres upwards in an event called subduction.

By the time they are monitoring it and relaying the information around the globe fifteen minutes later, the size of the bulge in the water has already increased to three metres.

Instead of being a wave in the true sense, the bulge is being created as result of the pressure of the water being pushed by the shock wave. A diver on the sea bed would see a conventional wave break above them if they were to look up. They would feel the force of the revolving movement of the water as they approached the surface.

An earthquake pressure wave feels more like the shock wave from an explosion to the same diver standing on the seabed. It would press their chest down momentarily and knock them off balance as the whole body of water around them moved.

As the pressure wave progresses into shallow water it rears up like a traditional tidal wave. By the time it reaches the shallow draft of the waters a few hundred metres from shore it is thirty metres high and roaring like an express train.

Iran doesn't benefit from the early warning sirens and evacuation procedures adopted along the coastline of Indonesia, Japan and the US. Since the advent of regular, deadly coastal events from the turn of the twenty-first century which began in Indonesia, when 230,000 people were killed and 1.7 million people were displaced, other nations have made sure they are prepared.

Not so Iran. There is little or no chance of preparing for the wall of water which is about to strike along their unsuspecting and unprepared coastline. American and Japanese tsunami technology doesn't extend to

Iran.

With a global network of HAARP arrays still pouring 15,000,000 watts of energy into the ionosphere above Iran and resonating at 2.5 ghz, the low frequency which scientists discovered triggered earthquakes, the initial 9.1 Magnitude shock equivalent to 100,000 atomic bombs is followed by dozens of further, slightly smaller tremors which send more and more shock waves after the initial giant.

They feed the wall of water which slams into the Iranian coastline and roars across the countryside to ensure the inundation doesn't let up. Coastal resorts, houses, cars, people, animals and vegetation are all demolished along hundreds of miles of coastline.

Iran's uranium enrichment plants like its oldest, the Bushehr Nuclear Plant built on the coast in the northwest end of the country, are not designed to withstand a twenty metre-high wave. Bushehr is under water within seconds. Most of its employees on site are immediately drowned or killed by debris in the water.

Originally built in the 1950s with the help of the US under the old US-friendly regime of the Shah of Iran, before he was deposed by the revolution, the plant is actually the secret primary target for Gates and the Brotherhood's covert attack. All the rest is a smokescreen.

The intention was for the plant to produce safe, clean electricity for Persia, as it was known then. But recently, its much-vaunted centrifuges have been producing plutonium with the acknowledged intention of building nuclear warhead which flies in the face of every international treaty.

The Brotherhood decided sanctions to stop production weren't enough. Just as they had with Japan and the Fukushima Nuclear plant which was found to be producing Plutonium for Iran.

The cooling pumps which prevent the reactor from overheating and going into meltdown stop working. The seawater, just as it had at the Fukushima plant, wrecks the backup batteries and generators housed in buildings destroyed by the shaking from the earthquakes. The temperature in the reactor is redlining within a few minutes.

As thousands drown or are crushed along 1200 kilometres of coastline, and a filthy, black viscous wave boils and bubbles across 30 miles of flat coastal land, the temperature is climbing dangerously high at the Bushehr plant. Within hours, the reactor will explode if it is left unchecked. Everyone who knows how it works is dead or injured and the chances of a major ecological disaster on top of the damage done by the tsunami increase with every passing minute.

They watch in silence on a TV in the edit suite as live news footage of the tsunami is broadcast on every channel. Trent, Rachel and Michael are back in handcuffs. Gates has managed to attach all three of them to metal safety rails around the fader console.

Shots of the black wave marching across the Iranian countryside destroying everything in its path are intercut with the smoking ruins of the Bushehr Nuclear plant. As they watch in silence, the dome of the reactor explodes and a white plume of steam and debris rockets skywards.

"There goes the neighbourhood," chuckles Gates insanely. "Time to release your big moment Trent."

"If you do that we are all dead," says Rachel in disbelief.

"You're all dead anyway. Time you realised that Rachel, my dear."

Gates looks triumphant as he presses a button marked 'Transmit'. Trent's pale, exhausted face appears on the tv screen.

"My name is Trent Richards. I am the leader of an organisation called Anonymous and my organisation is responsible for the destruction currently being delivered on Iran, our sworn enemy."

Rachel hisses at Gates, "How can you do that? How can you cut across a major network's output like that?"

"Friends in low places," crows Gates revelling in his moment of glory.

"Keep quiet. This is very good."

Michael appears unbothered by the profound horror of what is unfolding. In fact he is enjoying it as much as Gates.

Trent's impression in the video of a cold-hearted, ruthless powermonger is astonishingly convincing, even if it is born out of desperation.

The video, and Trent's impression of a terrorist, continues.

"The tsunami striking your coastline was triggered by a series of nuclear devices we detonated fifty kilometres from your coastline. The shock wave which resulted triggered a natural earthquake along the fault line which runs the length of the western side of your country. The plutonium for our bombs was smuggled out from under your noses from your own nuclear processing plant at Bushehr. It was rerouted from the illegal centrifuges there on its way to your own weapon makers. Material intended for nuclear warheads to be dropped on your neighbouring countries Israel, Japan,

North Korea and Russia."

Trent hesitates in the video and swallows nervously. His eyes dart to one side for an instant then return to the screen.

Trent reads his own involuntary movement as what it is—pressure and nerves. He prays others will see it and analyse it. He hopes beyond hope that someone will interpret the almost invisible twitch as a message and call it. He feels a pang of guilt for thinking about his own survival and his family at a time like this. Thousands of innocent people will have already died.

The explosion at Bushehr dwarfs Russia's famous nuclear disaster at Chernobyl, or Three Mile Island in the US or even Fukushima in Japan which didn't ever actually melt down and explode, unlike Chernobyl.

Bushehr was thought to have more than 100 tons of uranium deployed in the reactor which was the average for a nuclear power station. And now it had overheated when the cooling failed and exploded live on global television.

Trent's bogus confessional continues.

"Your biggest reactor, Bushehr in the north west, which America helped you build, has now exploded. The cloud of radioactive poison it is ejecting will cover your country and the Arab Peninsula. Our enemies will perish in the toxic cloud it is already producing and they will continue to die for years to come, long after the waters of the tsunami currently crushing your lands have receded."

"I particularly liked that part," Gates says proudly.

Trent, secretly dying inside, continues.

"This is our revenge on you for the evil deeds your country and your allies have done. It will stop the threat you pose to the free world for good and send out the strongest message possible to anyone else who thinks they can bomb their enemies into submission with no threat of reprisals."

The image of Trent vaporises and shots of the destruction still being wreaked on the Iranian coastline return. Trent and Rachel's faces are ashen.

"This is the end of the world," Rachel says numbly.

Within minutes, hastily thrown together reports on Trent's identity are beginning to appear in a media scrabble for an exclusive. They carry a surprising amount of accurate information about Trent and his military career, the helicopter crash in Afghanistan, Eli's background, and pictures of Rachel and Gareth. Speculation about Trent's motivation, his sanity and his political allegiances explodes across the media.

"Damn Google," Trent grunts ironically.

Gates tuts reproachfully.

"I think that worked perfectly. But now it's time to shut HAARP down. Firstly because I think they have got the message in a way they will never, ever forget and secondly we don't want them to work out how we really did it. It will be confusing enough for them when they find no evidence of the explosions although the fallout from their nuclear facilities should help muddy the waters almost literally."

At gunpoint, Gates releases each of them from their anchor points then makes them click the handcuffs around their own wrists.

Trent and Michael are thinking the same thing.

"Just him and us now. It's only a matter of time..."

Gates marches the three of them out of the edit suite into the corridor, just as the lights fail for the third time.

"It must have got dark outside again," observes Rachel as they stumble along in the near-darkness in the direction of the main control room.

"Why does that happen? He's just triggered a massive earthquake on the other side of the world. Surely there's enough power to run the lights at night?" asks Gareth.

Michael, in front of the three person line, turns his head and whispers out of Gates's hearing, "There are forces at work here which Gates doesn't understand. Far more powerful and dangerous in ways he and The Brotherhood can only dream of. The power of the Universe."

Trent shakes his head in the gloom.

"Whatever Michael, careful you don't trip."

Caught out by the sudden loss of light, they shuffle along the darkened corridor, bathed in the glow of the emergency luminous rings built into the overhead fittings. Trent keeps sight of Michael's blonde hair which appears to glow too. As they move along the corridor Trent catches the sound of something scuttling along in the air-conditioning vent above their heads.

"Did you hear that?" Trent hisses to no one in particular.

"Hear what?" replies Rachel, suddenly on edge.

"Just stop for a second and listen," urges Trent.

Gates jabs him in the small of his back with the Beretta.

"Why have you stopped? Keep moving or I'll shoot you now instead of later."

There's the scuttling sound again. Trent imagines a giant rat with long claws in the vent above them. It stops suddenly as if it is too listening.

"There's nothing there. Now stop playing for time and move."

Gates shoves Trent in the back and he stumbles forward into Rachel, who catches him by using her handcuffed arms as a scoop. Their eyes meet in the gloom.

"Good catch," observes Trent.

"I'll always be there for you Trent," replies Rachel, smiling.

In the control room, emergency back-up batteries maintain the myriad red glow of the indicator switches. Trent can see the systems are all still running despite the absence of the room lighting. Gates, in his paranoia, reverses the cuffing procedure until all three of them are locked to a solid metal fitting. Any chance of escape or turning on Gates who is now minus all four of his military retinue is zero.

Wordlessly, Gates throws various switches and levers. Lights blink out all over the fifteen metre-long console.

"Are you finally shutting that monstrosity off?" asks Trent.

"It's served its purpose for the time being," nods Gates, his back turned to Trent as he concentrates on the shutdown sequence.

"What about the others like the one in Costa Rica?" asks Michael.

Satisfied with his work, Gates leans back on the console and stretches his arms, folding his hands proprietorially around the edge of the desk as he does so.

"They will take their cue from my shutdown. We communicate with each other only when it is absolutely necessary for security. This facility is the master, all the others follow my actions automatically."

"It must be wonderful to have so much power," Rachel observes sarcastically.

Gates looks at Rachel as if he has just thought of something. A little housekeeping matter to address.

"Now I can concentrate there is something we need to do."

Keeping his unnerving, sadistic stare locked on Rachel, Gates goes to a metal storage cupboard, reaches in and produces the cruel, coiled whip he used on Robin then Gareth.

"We're going to conduct a little experiment. About revenge, anger and priorities."

"I don't like the sound of that, Gates," Trent says darkly.

"You are actually very good at picking up inference for such a stupid person. I'll put that down to base animal cunning."

Gates addresses the comment to Trent but keeps his cold, lizard-like eyes on Rachel. He looks her up and down, mentally undressing her. His eyes linger on her as he assesses the beautiful body she undoubtedly has under her torn, blood-stained clothes.

"Whatever you are thinking of doing, I wouldn't," Trent says.

"What we, or should I say you, is going to do is take this chance to punish your disgusting, adulterous slut of a wife for her wrongdoing which, correct me if I'm wrong, she has not exactly denied?"

Michael yanks his cuffed hands furiously.

"I warned you Gates. I gave you what you needed. You don't need to do this."

"Interesting isn't it how he can stand by and watch a whole country decimated but gets upset about one worthless whore," taunts Gates as he uncoils the whip and cracks it in the air.

He dangles the plaited leather cord in front of Rachel then slides it lasciviously between her breasts and traces the shape through her shirt with the tip.

"Sure I can't tempt you Trent? I know you want to. You're itching to under that English façade I feel sure."

Trent remains silent, staring with pure hatred at Gates as he taunts Rachel with the whip.

Gates arches one eyebrow.

"No? Pity."

"I'd rather die than comply with anything you want for another second. You are a demon. Probably Satan himself," states Trent flatly.

"Is that so?" asks Gates evenly, and then he casually shoots Trent in the thigh with the Beretta.

Trent screams in pain and collapses. He hangs from his handcuffed wrists as a crimson ring starts to spread outwards on the right thigh of his cargo pants.

"You are pathetic. You know she'll do it again and I have no doubt Michael here wasn't the first time. I'll just have to do it for you. For all the other gullible, weak fools who have been blinded by women's lies dressed as love."

Gates raises the whip and lands an expert lash across Rachel's back. With a huge effort of will, she holds in the scream of pain she wants to emit.

"Leave her alone you fucking madman. If you want to hurt someone, hurt me," gasps Trent.

"That bargaining chip didn't work with your son and it won't work with the slut," Gates replies, panting slightly.

He raises the whip once again and lands another blow across Rachel's belly and thigh. This time she shrieks in pain.

There is a sudden, deafening explosion.

Trent sees a small red hole appear in Gates's forehead. The demonic look of sadistic glee is frozen on his face as he tips forward and crashes to the ground. The back of his head has been blown off and his brains are spread all over his black, greasy hair.

As Gates drops out of Trent's eyeline, he sees Robin standing in the doorway unsteadily clasping a snub-nosed Smith and Wesson 38. It has a wisp of acrid gun smoke curling upwards from the barrel. Gareth, his upper torso strapped tightly with lumpy field dressings and bandages, is in his wheelchair next to Robin.

"I said I'd get you, bitch." Robin keeps the gun raised in her shaking hands as her eyes sweep the room for any other hostile targets.

Trent sobs with relief.

"Robin, thank God. He was going to kill us all. Help Rachel for me, please."

Robin pushes the 38 into a black Dupont side holster strapped to her thigh. She steps behind Gareth and slides a three foot long set of bolt cutters from the pouch on the back of his wheelchair and sets about Rachel's handcuffs. The cuffs pop off and clatter to the floor.

"Thanks babe," Rachel says as she rubs her wrists.

"Let me see your back."

Robin starts to gently raise Rachel's shirt.

"She's an expert Rachel. Look what she did to me." Gareth's familiar flat intonation cuts through the silence. "I think my dad urgently needs something to help stop that bleeding though."

Gareth's eyes go to Trent who is hanging from the cuffs and is barely conscious. His cargo pants are soaked red.

Robin touches Rachel's arm compassionately.

"I need to help Trent."

Rachel nods and pushes her away. Robin cuts through Trent's cuffs with ease and he slumps to the floor. She places the bolt cutters against the front of the console between him and Michael with one hand and tentatively feels around the wound through hole in the material. She runs her hand around the opposite side of his leg and finds what she is looking for. An exit wound.

"You're in luck Trent. The bullet passed clean through you. There may be some fragments still in there and they, along with everything else, are going to set off an infection. We need to get a tourniquet going."

Robin takes the whip from where it landed on the floor and winds it around Trent's upper leg just below his. She ties the ends around the wooden handle. She twists it and Trent cries out. He slumps back and almost loses consciousness. Robin studies his face as she winds another turn into the make-shift tourniquet.

"Gotta slow the blood loss somehow. Sorry it hurts but it's a whole lot better than bleeding out. Can you hold it?"

Robin presses Trent's hand down on the wooden handle which has turned from a light ash colour to black as it is soaked in Trent's blood.

"I can do it," Trent says though gritted teeth.

Robin turns to face where Michael should still be attached to the console but he has disappeared. His cuffs are lying on the floor next to the cutters. She shrugs and turns back to attend to Trent.

Rachel moves over to join them and leans close to her husband.

"We need to get out of here Trent or we will never leave," she whispers into his blood-encrusted ear.

Trent nods then leans back in exhaustion and closes his eyes. He covers her hand with his.

# Michael

Gareth whirrs away down the corridor to look for Michael. His wheelchair lights pick out the rough surface of the breeze-blocks until he comes to the open door of the edit suite. He stops, uncertain what to do next. Michael might be hiding in there and then he is going to have to deal with that.

Can I trust him? He thinks to himself. I want to, despite what he and Rachel did. He'd learned a lot about being an adult in the last three days and it wasn't as easy as it looked he'd realised.

Gareth is startled out of his thought process by a strange scratching coming from the air-conditioning duct. It sounds like the claws of a large animal as the sources of the scratching and clattering are some way apart from each other—maybe two metres as far as he can tell.

Hearing the eerie, inexplicable sound propels Gareth into the familiar, relative security of the edit suite. He's learned the castle and the bunker below it are a weird and dangerous place. A kind of hell on earth and both so far have shown little or no respite. A rat or whatever is in the air conditioning and it's the size of a man. That is not going to be a good thing.

The VCR Gareth originally found in the edit suite has reappeared in exactly the same place he found it. Odd. A suddenly functioning Humvee and now the camera has found its way back to here. Is it possible time has folded back on itself like Michael said it might?

Using the pencil beams from the LED lights built into the wheelchair arm rests, Gareth inspects the camera. It's definitely the same one. The viewfinder is extended. It's broken and blackened in exactly the same way. It was on the breakfast island in the kitchen the last time he saw it. Maybe someone brought it down again at some stage. But who?

For some reason his interest is piqued as if the camera is trying to flag up something for his attention. Always the curious, enquiring mind, Gareth extends the titanium probe from the right arm of his wheelchair and prods around the camera until he successfully depresses the play button on the side.

There is a momentary flash on the little cracked screen then what is now the familiar sight of the interrogation room appears where Gates flogged Gareth until he almost killed him.

Rafael, the skinny Italian with long hair and Gabriela, the rather overweight Australian woman, are sitting in chains. They are wearing the same badly-fitting orange Guantanamo Bay style overalls they were in the first time Gareth saw them. It seems so long ago since he saw them the first time.

Rafael and Gabriela are being interrogated by an unseen man who identifies himself as Colonel Hassan. They say they are activists like Michael. Colonel Hassan accuses them of being Israeli Mossad Secret Service spies.

The interrogation becomes heated very quickly. Colonel Hassan is very aggressive. There are threats and shouting. A metal pole is slammed on the metal surface of the interrogation table by Hassan, making the captives jump so violently in their seats that the chains attaching them to the table yank tight.

Despite Hassan's aggressive questioning, Rafael and Gabriela are stubbornly tight-lipped about their identities and the name of their organisation. The threats and abuse reach a crescendo and they start to yell in protest at the way they are being treated. Furious and afraid, Gabriela suddenly spits out: "Michael is no activist, he is something else altogether".

Something much more dangerous.

Rafael and Gabriela seem really afraid of even mentioning Michael's name. Much more afraid even than they are of their interrogator.

He asks them exactly what they mean.

"He is a demon," says Gabriela.

"Worse than that," says Rafael, "he is THE demon. Abbadon, the beast of the pit, the only entity to have ever captured Satan."

They are babbling now. Dribbling spittle and shedding tears of terror.

"Michael can conjure horrible beasts and demons. He kills constantly purely for the fun of it. And he takes the soul of everyone he kills to eternal damnation," shouts Gabriela.

"He is a liar, a false prophet. He twists everything and everyone around his little finger. He will kill you Hassan. He will most certainly kill us. There is no escape. We've seen what he's done. Everyone here is doomed already."

Rafael's eyes are wild and the size of saucers. His hands have started to shake uncontrollably.

There is a pause and then Hassan laughs out long and loud. He claps slowly, mocking them.

"Very good. No, really. You are either the best

trained operatives or utter idiots. The end result is the same though. You have been caught trespassing and most likely spying. You will never leave prison as it is so you may as well tell me the truth, not this nonsense."

There is the sound of a chair scraping back then a creak as it takes his weight as he sits down. Hassan has been standing throughout the interrogation. A match is struck as he lights a cigarette. He inhales, and then exhales noisily.

"What were you doing throwing your lives away for such an evil and malevolent specimen? Assuming you're not all spies of course?" asks Hassan quizzically.

Rafael and Gabriela look at each other nervously. Rafael nods. Gabriela turns to face her interrogator.

"We are fallen angels. Michael was an archangel and he took his name from Archangel Michael. Although that is most definitely not who he is. He is not the severer of evil attachments and the guardian of children like the real Michael. We are compelled to do his bidding."

She stares at Hassan for a few moments then drops her head in either resignation or shame.

Gareth has a horrible crawling knot of fear in his stomach. After the supernatural, murderous events of the last three days, he is ready to believe anything.

Hassan sighs wearily. Rafael is staring blankly at something. He could be looking at Hassan. Gareth can't tell as Hassan is behind the camera, unseen.

"OK. Let's humour you for a second and accept you are spacemen or something. But that still doesn't explain what you are doing here?"

Gabriela raises her head again and sets her jaw.

"Michael is attracted to power and this place has the most powerful thing man has ever stumbled on. It's the same power which brought the Universe into existence thirteen billion years ago. It is the God particle. The spark of omnipotent intelligence, consciousness, call it what you like."

Rafael snaps out of the trancelike state he had fallen into.

"God meant technology like HAARP in its natural state to be used for peaceful and constructive ends like the way the Sumerians, Atlanteans, Pharoahs, Incas and the Gnostics used it. Michael was drawn here because of the opportunity for destruction. He adores chaos, disorder and suffering. He loves creating hell. It's what he does."

Gabriela adds, "He is the Fallen One, father of the Watchers, and the Nephilim after that. The Ark of the Covenant used the same technology, or magic, depending on your viewpoint, as what you know as HAARP. Michael finally stole the Ark from God's angels to prevent his enemies ever winning another battle against him. The earth and the whole Universe has been in decline ever since. We are approaching the end game now."

Hassan clears his throat.

"Let me get this straight. All these ancient civilisations took turns to possess the Ark. To win their battles against your friend Michael?" he asks.

Gabriela nods furiously.

"Yes, yes, all those battles. The battle of good against evil. God against the Devil. The one which started in the Book of Genesis and continued into the Book of Enoch. Where God's angels chased Archangel Lucifer and his rebellious followers out of heaven and condemned them to the pit."

Rafael interrupts. "Archangel Gabriel took pity on

them and threw his golden magic lyre into the pit so they would have the music of angels to give them respite from their eternal suffering. But eventually Lucifer escaped and now walks the earth with Gabriel's lyre. It can draw angels who have slipped from his power to their doom. And Satan wants every single one of his wicked fallen angels back."

"And you two are fallen angels?" sneers Hassan.

Gabriela and Rafael suddenly gasp with fear but it's nothing to do with their cynical, antagonistic interrogator. Their mouths work but no sound comes out, except for a strangled, terrified sobbing.

"You can ask him yourself," Gabriela finally manages. "He's standing right behind you."

There is a slow, devilish growling from what sounds like an animal of some kind. The same spine-chilling snarl Gareth has heard more than he ever wants to again. There is a shrill, high-pitched bubbling scream as Colonel Hassan dies horribly. Mercifully, the carnage is unseen by the camera. There are just the sounds. It does however capture Gabriela and Rafael's look of abject, catatonic fear.

Blood spurts across their frozen white, sweating faces. Suddenly, there is another unearthly shriek and a dark shadow blinks across the screen. Then the image disappears. Nothing remains apart from static and a loud hissing noise.

Gareth stares blankly in front of him. Then he realises that Michael is standing silently behind him in the doorway.

Satan is right there in the room with him and he is all alone with the most evil being in the Universe.

"Did you see that?" asks Gareth through the vocoder.

"See what?" asks Michael innocently, lightly.

Gareth blinks the reverse command on his wheelchair and it rolls back and collects Michael, catching him unawares. Michael is pinned against the door. Gareth keeps the momentum on and the wheels skid impotently on the shiny floor. To Gareth's surprise, Michael doesn't resist. He clings to the back of the chair and tries to prevent it from toppling over as it bounces and bucks around wildly.

"Gareth! Please stop! Stop it! I am not your enemy! I am Archangel Michael. That much is true. I am your protector. And I need you. Please!...Listen to me. I am not what you think I am. You have it all wrong. Gabriela and Rafael were the demons, not me. That's what demons do. That thing came to claim its own. They trick you! Please—listen to me!"

Gareth finally relents and releases Michael who falls forward on his hands and knees.

In between gasps Michael says, "I have been protecting you Gareth. You couldn't possibly realise it but you are the Guardian of the Ark Of The Covenant. Its energy is *your* energy. You were born with it and have been incarnated with it in many lives before. It is your soul. *That's* where it's been hidden since the beginning of time. That's where I hid it. Yes. Me. Not in a parallel time like I pretended to Gates. If he'd known he would have killed you. That's where I hid it so Satan would never find it again and use it as a weapon. I did it on the Lord God's bidding as he is my Master and I worship no other."

Gareth spins his wheelchair round so Michael is directly in front where he can see him properly.

"Why now Michael? Why wait all this time. Not that I believe you anyway by the way."

"This man-made place we are in and the energy they have harnessed with the HAARP machine drew you down here. You could feel the energy couldn't you? What Gates didn't realise, *couldn't* realise, is the terrible danger they have put the human race in by starting to use it. It is the power of the Ark. The power of the Ark is infinite, it is what was used to create time and space and it can just as easily end it. Which was why I had to hide that vessel, that energy. And I hid it in your soul. It is a gift of the most unimaginable proportions. But the key to access it is too powerful. It's what robbed you of your ability to communicate with the outside world.

Gareth's eyes are glistening with tears.

"We need to get away from here immediately. If we can transfer the key to the Ark, you will return to how you remember when you were a little boy. You will be able to walk, to swim in the ocean, make love. We must travel to South America to a descendant of the Mayan race I have identified who is the only other soul on this planet of more than seven billion who is suitable to receive the key.

"Will the same thing happen to her that happened to me?" Gareth asks.

Michael looks annoyed by the interruption.

"No. She is from the Council of Galactic Elders originally. She is far more evolved than you and her soul will deal with the power better than you. She is ready to receive the Key from you but you must connect physically to transfer it successfully. And you will be released from your bodily prison. All the functions associated with moving, touching, speaking, the physical will be yours. Just like an angel incarnated. A watcher. A Nephilim. An angel made flesh. Just like us. How does that sound to you?"

Michael stops, seemingly exhausted.

Gareth's eyes don't leave Michael's face. His rapid breathing begins to slow.

"You can really do all that?" asks Gareth though the flat emotion of the voice synthesiser.

Michael looks earnestly at him. "Yes."

"OK. We'll go. Dad won't like it though," says Gareth through the voice synthesiser.

Gareth's hazel eyes bathed in the greenish hue of his high-tech eyepiece and Michael's unearthly blue ones lock and there is a long moment of silence.

Michael breaks the spell.

"We don't have to tell him. You don't know it yet but you may have just saved yourself and the whole human race, Gareth. Bless you my child. You are an extraordinary person. Let's muster the others and get away from this evil place as soon as we can."

Trent appears behind Michael in the corridor, supported with difficulty by Robin and Rachel. His face is ashen and there are brown semi-circles under his eyes from the blood loss.

Gareth pushes past Michael who is blocking the doorway.

"We're going. Now."

Gareth, with Rachel and Robin stumbling awkwardly under Trent's weight, make for the elevator. Michael hurries ahead.

# Endgame

As they emerge on the ground floor, Michael steps out of the elevator behind Gareth and the others, then stops and presses the down button. The empty elevator hums almost silently back to the basement as the survivors above stagger out into the dawn light.

Michael opens the door of the mud-covered Humvee and hits the ignition switch. Its windows are opaque from the coating of dirt it has picked up from chasing across the mountain looking for Gareth. The huge vehicle roars into life and a thick cloud of diesel fumes is ejected from the exhaust at the rear.

Rachel and Robin cheer. Michael gives them the thumbs-up. With some extra help from Michael, they lever Trent into the back. He's too weak to climb in and they have to push him up.

Gareth hangs back in the castle doorway under the grumpy Gargoyle. He watches as Robin and Rachel clamber in after Trent, who is slumped across the wide rear seat. Michael, who seems to have forgotten something, jogs back round the Humvee, straight past Gareth and into the castle.

As they settle in the back Rachel wrinkles up her finely-shaped nose at the filthy state of the vehicle.

"This is going to be job for the carwash boys like they've never had before. You can't even see out the windows."

Michael runs as fast as he can to the elevator and slides to a halt. The indicator light on the control switch shows it is on the way back up.

He stands aside and opens his arms wide. He closes his eyes and tilts his head back. A deep, unearthly growl comes out of his wide snarl of a mouth.

Gareth starts to move forward in his wheelchair to join the others. A familiar sound comes from somewhere behind the Humvee. Gareth stops his wheelchair, frozen. Growling. A deep, slow, terrifying, resonating rumble of an animal growling.

"Get out. All of you. Get out. Right now!"

But no-one can hear him. His flat, synthesised voice is swallowed in the loud, low exhaust of the Humvee.

Gareth's eyes are fixed on the silhouettes of his friend and parents through the mud-covered windows. Suddenly there is an explosion of ripping and snarling activity in the Humvee over terrified screams.

Blood and fleshy body parts are hurled against the misted-up windows. A hand splays against a window and slides down, leaving a dark shadow of blood on the glass. The snarling fury of the unseen demonic beast slaughtering Gareth's whole world rocks the Humvee on its axis.

At that moment, the first shafts of bright morning light hit the side of the vehicle and the dreadful sounds stop as suddenly as they started.

Gareth is unable to think or react. His eyes are wide and flooded with hot, wet tears. A thin, monotone scream starts and builds in volume. Then it becomes a human scream, a real, agonised scream.

And it is coming from Gareth. His own voice. His mouth is open and he is venting all the pain, horror and anger in the world.

The sound of Gareth's voice is cut dead by an explosion which rips through the Humvee. Gareth is rocked in his wheelchair by the force. A fireball mushrooms skywards and burning, smoking debris sprinkles down on Gareth unchecked.

Very slowly he turns the wheelchair on its axis.

Michael is standing right behind him. Untouched, unperturbed, calm.

"It's just you and me now Gareth. You, me and the power of the Universe."

"MURDERER!" shouts Gareth, his lips and lower jaw forming the words. He launches forward against Michael's legs, knocks him down and keeps going. A wheel bounces over Michael's leg and catches on the material of his trousers, dragging him slowly along the ground.

Gareth drags Michael toward the elevator in a surreal, slow motion pirouette. Michael realises what Gareth is planning and struggles to free his leg. He is shouting in a strange, guttural alien language. His once benign and handsome angelic face is distorted by a mask of hatred, evil and fury.

Gareth reaches the open safety cage of the elevator, tears streaming down his newly-mobile face. The front wheels of his wheelchair catch for an instant on the metal lip of the elevator entrance. Then with a final spurt he tips into the darkness, dragging Michael with him. But the elevator has gone again and they drop together out of sight.

Silence. There is a loud crash, then silence again.

Outside, the flames from the Humvee have almost

died down, leaving a charred, burnt-out metal carcass. There is no sign of the others in the wreckage.

Against a background of low, crackling flames and the ticking of cooling metal, the dawn chorus abruptly starts as if a switch has been thrown.

In the distance down the long drive a Mercedes Traveliner people carrier is approaching. As it draws closer, Trent, Rachel, Ted, Gareth and the others are clearly in view. They roll to a stop near the burnt-out wreck of the Humvee and get out.

The beautiful, rippling sound of a lyre rises and falls in pitch from somewhere deep in the castle.

8805374R00125

Printed in Great Britain
by Amazon.co.uk, Ltd.,
Marston Gate.